Bit on the Side:

Work, sex, love, loss and own goals

Anna Kiernan is a writer, editor and lecturer. She has written for various publications and is currently working on a PhD at Goldsmiths, on the subject of James Joyce, coincidence and life writing.

Bit on the Side:

Work, sex, love, loss and own goals

Edited by Anna Kiernan

Parthian
The Old Surgery
Napier Street
Cardigan
SA43 1ED

www.parthianbooks.co.uk

First published in 2007
© The authors 2007
This collection © Parthian 2007
All Rights Reserved

ISBN 978-1-905762-05-7

Editors: Gwen Davies and Anna Kiernan

Cover design by Eleanor Rose
Cover photograph by Sam Rogg
Inner design by books@lloydrobson.com
Printed and bound by Gwasg Gomer, Llandysul, Wales

Published with the financial support of the Welsh
Books Council.

British Library Cataloguing in Publication Data

A cataloguing record for this book is available from
the British Library.

Contents

3. Borderline

4. La Vie en Rose

5. Don't Explain

Introduction

The women whose writing appears in the pages that follow are in many respects exceptional personalities, but that is not what connects them here. They are linked instead by the typical character of the stories they tell, because each tale contains a revelation or a dilemma that many women have faced or will face at some time in their lives. They also, incidentally, share a loose geographical and cultural connection with Wales.

While it is not a sequel or a postscript, this book consciously echoes another, written twenty years ago and edited by Valerie Grove. As Mavis Nicholson explains in her contribution 'Loved to Distraction', *The Compleat Woman: Marriage, Motherhood, Career: Can she have it all?* drew together writing by half a dozen women exceptional in their ways but united by experiences common to many. *Bit on the Side* takes a similar approach but explores different territory,

1

charting some of the changes, challenges, frustrations and jubilations experienced by modern (or postmodern) women.

It is divided into five sections, which are partially collated according to the stage of life to which they refer, but also to the mood of the pieces, so that the three pieces in the first section, 'State of Independence', talk, at least in part, about childhood, and the realisation of difference, or of *being different*, during childhood.

In 'John Lennon Spoke to Me' Hayley Long recalls the moment when it became apparent that her musical taste was out of step with her peers, at the age of nine, when she played the song 'Woman is the nigger of the world' in her needlework class. Setting the stage for later trials and tribulations as a DJ, Hayley's battle even then was with mindless pop, since her classmates and teacher were, she discovered, much more comfortable singing along to Abba's inane cry of 'Su-pa-pa, Troo-pa-pa!'

Layla's teenage struggles, after a childhood spent on a commune with her Scottish/Iraqi parents, focused on her desire to play football professionally: *I am really short; I read Bryan Robson's autobiography which said he was too. The way he dealt with it was to drink Guinness and raw egg in the morning – it couldn't make him taller but it could make him stronger. So I started doing that. Tina and John bought me Guinness in the weekly shop when I was about fifteen, so I used to have the same as Bryan Robson every morning before school.*

'From This Day Forth', recalls Holly Howitt being forced prematurely to consider her status as an independent woman, when a class bully told her, at the age of five, that she had to get married, because 'it's the law!': *I think about my role models, searching for the truth. She-Ra isn't married. But Bow is chasing* after her, I know that. I have the doll version of Bow and you can make his heart beat when She-Ra comes near by pushing in a little button at his spine. Tales of Abba, Guinness and She-ra, are perhaps quite naturally the preoccupations of these three young women, whose vocations now are as a DJ, footballer and writer.

The second section, 'Equally Cursed and Blessed', is about becoming a woman. That probably sounds a bit too 'Cixous' for a collection like this, but what I mean is that these pieces are about the disparity between how we thought it would be (being a grown-up, that is), 'how life is' and how we can shape our own destinies through our decisions. This section speaks of the highs and lows of love and other drugs and the peculiar expectations of our sex to tolerate the intolerable and accept our fate without complaint.

In the eponymously titled 'Bit on the Side' Robyn ap Gwilym tests out her assertion that she is a feminist through a discussion of her affair with a married man and through observations of the often unfulfilled lives of those who 'have it all'. She says: *I am someone who has always been in and out of love, who is accustomed to being wanted; the school cheerleader type. I know my charms but it may be that I am addicted to a certain sort of thrill. It may be that coming from a family repeatedly reinvented, broken and extended makes laughable the notion of merely "you and I".*

Reflecting on the devastating events that took place after a night out in Swansea in the 1970s, when she was a teenager, Jo Mazelis' powerful account of a lucky twist of fate is also a diatribe about a woman's right to live without the fear of sexual intimidation. In 'Before the Rain' she describes the 'flashers' that she and her best friend were forced to endure,

3

with a description that is at once humane, poetic and repugnant: *And then there was his penis: a flaccid, pink, alien thing offered in the palm of his hand as if it were a gift or something to be inspected; a butcher showing his best pork sausages for the housewife's approval, the child with a flower.*

Sadie Kiernan's account of being seduced by Ecstasy during the early nineties is an affectionate portrait of a sub-culture, written by someone who has suffered its downside but still wryly reminisces about experiencing a chemically enhanced version of reality. As an insulin-dependent diabetic, Sadie was particularly susceptible to the negative effects of both the drugs and her lifestyle. The havoc the highs and lows played with her blood sugar levels may have contributed to the decline of her health and the deterioration of her kidney function (which resulted in her being on dialysis for several years and having a successful kidney-pancreatic transplant two years ago). Or it may not have. Although reflective about her raving years, Sadie says, *I don't regret these phenomenal experiences and how some dimension of my perception remains perpetually influenced by them.*

From raves on Pembrokeshire beaches, Rachel Trezise's 'Dumping Stucky' takes readers to the grim but darkly comic reality of the Rhondda (and her boyfriend Stucky) from which, as a teenager, she was so keen to escape: *In 1999 I turned twenty. I still lived in the Rhondda and the Rhondda was the same place it had always been.... What I saw was obese women who thought nothing of shopping in their pyjamas and teenagers on hard drugs... it was a decade since my stepfather had raped me and six years since he was found not guilty.*

Both Sadie (who is my sister) and Rachel's tales of mis-spent youths, despite dismissing any form of sentimentalism, reveal an underlying desire for escapism, both literal and psychological. The strength of both writers lies in their dark humour and ability to observe the absurdity of human behaviour so astutely. In 'Dumping Stucky', Rachel outlines the inauspicious beginnings of her romance with Stucky, a recovering addict: *A month before I'd left, I'd met a new boyfriend in the local pub. There was a darts match on, and they had a buffet. He had winked at me over the left-over faggot sandwiches.*

The third section, 'Borderline', opens with Patricia Duncker's account of passing over the Welsh border in the dead of night, before switching to a spot-in-time in Germany, some years before, when, like Cinderella, she missed her midnight deadline for returning to the Berlin wall, so enraptured was she by watching *Faust*. The performance, Duncker explains, was, *...about wanting more, more of everything, more knowledge, more youth, more sex, more life.* This section, then, is partly about the struggle to embrace independence rather than fearing it. And the desire to take risks. In 'Teithio yn y Nos Nachtreise' Duncker says, *One of the great recurring clichés in contemporary women's fiction is that tension evident in the desire for radical independence and yet the need to remain in the relative safety of home.* Fiction, its narratives and its closures, are a recurrent preoccupation in this collection in which women are seeking out truths to match their desires and experiences (no doubt because many of the writers here are first and foremost novelists).

In 'The Splinter of Ice' Liz Jones speaks of the ambivalence she felt in the 1980s in Thatcher's London, as a feminist, mother and evictee. *What feminism hadn't prepared me for... was the overwhelming love I was to feel for my baby. Those*

5

sublime mother-and-baby moments, the heart-stopping smiles and gurgles that were to play havoc with my postnatal hormones. That was when a voice would whisper, beg me not to do it – not to leave her. Then another voice – a loud, strident one – would interrupt, order me to go out and earn money, save up, buy a house, don't get left behind.

Such cultural and gendered schizophrenia is commonplace in *Bit on the Side*, which can perhaps be seen as an indication of a wider sense of the divided self among women in society generally. As Robyn ap Gwilym explains: *There is a notion in feminist constructivist thinking that women have historically been "split" – they view themselves as subject and object, because they are accustomed to being objectified by the male gaze or, more accurately, the patriarchal gaze.*

So *Bit on the Side*, and this section in particular, is explicitly about cultural shifts and tensions, jarring expectations and frustrations and the possibility of moving almost effortlessly, as Caryl Lewis suggests, between borders. *I know some young women who feel disenfranchised from their identity and find themselves living in quite a schizophrenic state, being at once educated liberated twenty-somethings of the Bellini-drinking variety and making domestic contributions to farms and homes as such domestic duties are felt by them and those around them to be a highly prized contribution to the home economy.* 'Borderline' is about ideas of nationality and belonging, womanhood and Welshness. The ambivalence of this section is present throughout the book but it is here that it is mapped out geographically. In a sense it is the most acute measure of the anthology's title – since these women are writing about their experiences of cultural hybridity – of being interlopers in Wales or outsiders beyond its borders. (And Wales, of course, is the 'bit on the side' of England, the country that was its coloniser.) As Catherine Johnson observes, after a lifetime of being a Welsh Jamaican Londoner, *I'll never be white so I'll never be Welsh. It's that simple.*

The mood shifts in 'La Vie en Rose' to one of celebration, with Carol Lee suggesting that, *At a time when we are encouraged schizophrenically to re-invent ourselves at will, celebration is a force for stability. An adult affair, that says we are human beings with histories, which are what we hold onto in dark times.* It is in this section that an other-worldly element is introduced, through Charmian Savill's duplicitous domestic goddess and Rose Wilkins' fairy ancestry.

'La Vie en Rose' shows the compensatory potential of the imagination – and reminds us of the need to question doctrines which we did not originate, and to laugh often at ourselves and also at the over-earnest. Here, Charmian Savill conjures incarnations of herself in the Shakespearean characters of 'Prosperina' and Ariel (who are, respectively, the worrying and placating personas), as she prepares a feast at a pivotal moment in her life. Her desire is to infuse the proceedings with the sensual pleasures of her food, so when the Bush/Blair relationship causes conversational consternation around the dinner table, she decides it is time for afters: *Pudding. A rich chocolate Spanish torte with orange ice-cream, surrounded by a smooth, alcoholic orange custard. Sweetens the dynamic, and then it erupts. Four-letter expletives land all over the table like discarded shuttlecocks.*

Rose Wilkins, editor and author of teenage chick-lit, begins her piece by saying, *I was about six when I was first told I was descended from a fairy.* What's more, she can prove it! What cannot be proved, she is quick to point out, are the

7

rather darker imaginings of more enlightened thinkers: *Just before I began to write this piece, research by Susan Darker-Smith, a graduate student in behavioural psychotherapy, was widely reported in the press as claiming that early exposure to fairy tales subliminally encourages girls to grow up into victims of domestic violence.... Which is a theory that demonstrates as much common sense as a poultice of peacock dung, frankly.*

It is Rose who poses the question that niggles so many of my generation: *You can be a feminist who loves fairy stories, but can you be a feminist who writes chick-lit? I wish I could decide.* Voicing the tension that is as relevant in the 'Noughties as Betty Friedan's discussion of 'the problem that has no name' in her early 1960s classic, *The Feminine Mystique*, Wilkins muses that, *My upbringing and education were at pains to teach me that success is not kissing a handsome prince, virtue is not a pretty face, and happiness is not a combination of the two. Aged thirteen, I didn't believe it. Aged twenty-six I do – about 75% of the time. That other 25% is distracted by the aspirational neuroses celebrated by popular culture....*

And finally, 'Don't Explain', which is made up of two pieces about unexpected love and unimaginable loss. Here, Mavis Nicholson speaks of the phase of life she now finds herself in: *A lot of people have asked, "Aren't you scared?" But I'm not scared. When Geoff died, the worst thing that could happen to me had happened and I guess I wasn't scared of anything after that. I don't like it but I know, to some extent, I am coping with being on my own at seventy-four years of age.* Anne Rowe speaks of a different sort of loss in her piece, 'Love Bade Me Welcome', perhaps one of the most poignantly romantic stories in the collection. She begins, *My mother was seventy-nine when I came along.* Her mother being Eiddwen,

Rowe's new next door neighbour at her weekend retreat in Wales. *That my mother loved me I'm sure, but she was nearing forty when I was born, and was never able to express her love in the way Eiddwen is able to.*

Bit on the Side is not about happy endings – after all it isn't fiction. Nor is it an attempt to summarise 'what women want'. Rather it is about how sixteen women (ranging from their 20s to their 70s) feel about what they have, and what they might have, or might have had. Like Hesiod's Greek myth, contained here, beneath the various song titles attributed to each section are the five ages (which I hasten to note are symbolic rather than literal) of woman.

Estelle C Jelinek, editor of *Women's Autobiography: Essays in Criticism*, observes that, *the consensus among critics is that a good autobiography not only focuses on its author but also reveals his connectedness to the rest of society; it is representative of his times, a mirror of his era.* 'Connectedness' can be taken to mean our domestic setups, family difficulties, romances, ideals and influences – it is, perhaps, a notion bound up in daily life rather than abstract ideals.

Ambivalence is a thread that runs through this collection. The very title, 'bit on the side' is contentious in certain ways, signifying, as it does, something or someone peripheral. Perhaps it is time to reclaim the term for women, who have historically been tarred with the title 'a bit on the side'. I hope that this anthology goes some way towards doing that – with ambivalence, certainly, but also with the sort of optimism and passion that informs each of the stories in this book.

Anna Kiernan, September 2006

1

State of Independence

John Lennon Spoke to Me

Hayley Long

When I was nine years old, my teacher asked me to bring some music into school. After much head-scratching, the tape I eventually chose was *Shaved Fish* by John Lennon. But within minutes of the music starting, it became clear that Miss Ellsworthy didn't like it. In fact, she was quite obviously struggling right from the opening lyrical assault of *Give Peace a Chance*. Her patience finally wore out just before the end of side one and she decisively pressed the Stop button. Amidst all the uncertainties that shroud every detail of my past, there is one point of which I am absolutely sure: I will never forget the name of the song that finally broke her. It was called *Woman is the Nigger of the World*.

Allow me to explain. In 1980, I didn't own a very wide selection of music cassettes and records. In fact, I owned precisely six pre-recorded music tapes and zero vinyl records.

Of the six cassettes, four were so shameful that they didn't even count:

Wally Whyton Sings Your Favourite Nursery Rhymes
More Nursery Rhymes With Wally
Sing-a-long With Rolf Harris
Even More Nursery Rhymes With Wally.

If my friends had known of the existence of such items, they would have laughed at me forever. Which left just Shakin' Stevens who I no longer liked or *The Very Best of Johnny Cash* which my granddad had given me. I'd listened to the latter once and then, haunted by his gravelly axe-murderer's voice and joyless ballads about death, had spent several weeks only able to sleep with the light on.

So when Miss Ellsworthy cheerily announced to all the girls in my class that we could each take turns bringing in some music for everyone to enjoy during needlework lessons, she probably never fully comprehended quite how much pressure she was placing me under. I'm sure she thought she was doing a good thing. The music was intended as a special treat – a sweetener perhaps, to stem the rise of insurgency which had been growing among the more rebellious girls for several days. Some of us, myself included, had expressed a desire to forego the pleasures of the cross-stitch pyjama-case-making to join the boys outside who were making model aeroplanes with Mr Meadows. Miss Ellsworthy had said that this was impossible. When I had asked why, she had said 'Because you are a girl'. The rebel within me didn't stretch as far as answering back to a teacher so I had quietly accepted this. For the record, I think she was wrong to judge my state of femaleness as a barrier to the high and manly art of paper folding, but even so, it should not be forgotten that she was a good person. She was young and modern and had a big flicky-fringe and wore lots of blue eye make-up and when Julie had brought in The Nolans and Kate had brought in David Essex she had impressed us all by nodding her head and tapping her feet in time to the music while we all got on resignedly with our cross-stitch pyjama-cases.

So when it came to my turn, I was in a quandary. What would I take in? How could I leap over this crucial social hurdle and survive the harsh judgement of my peers? More importantly, how was I going to make Miss Ellsworthy tap her foot with only Johnny Cash and Wally Whyton to choose from? The answer came from my dad. 'Choose one of mine,' he had said generously, saving my world from collapse, 'borrow whatever you like.' This was no mean offer. My dad's music collection was massive. He had tapes *and* records, all neatly sorted and stored and I had been granted permission to choose whatever I wanted. As I recall, there was so much choice, it had all been a little overwhelming. After much deliberation, I had somehow managed to narrow it down to three:

Toyah! Toyah! Toyah! by Toyah
The Best of the Spinners
Shaved Fish by John Lennon.

In truth, all I really knew about the latter was that it was my dad's most recent purchase. Examining the tape's inlay card had not helped me much either. Whereas the other two albums on my shortlist were fronted by the standard fuzzy-focus portraits I had come to expect, on *Shaved Fish* John Lennon was nowhere to be seen. Instead, there was a drawing of a naked woman with a veil over her head crawling perilously on her hands and knees as she avoided missiles shaped like giant lipsticks. I was baffled by this and almost put the cassette back on the shelf but then I remembered that John Lennon was a genius and hesitated. I knew he was because my dad had told me. And what's more, my dad had never said anything about The Spinners or Toyah being geniuses. I plumped for *Shaved Fish*.

I must have missed the word *Nigger* in the track-listing. If I had spotted it, it would, without a doubt, have ruined the entire album for me. As much as I loved The Beatles, I was also uncomfortably aware of their 'difficult' side. The side which clouded over my perfect pop image and spoilt things. I liked to picture my four heroes as clean, lovable mop-tops who sang clean, cheerful pop songs about holding hands. And, unlike the scary pairing of John and Yoko, they kept their clothes firmly on. At nine years old, I carefully edited the naked bits and the hairy bits and the tuneless bits out of their careers and stuck doggedly to the bits I liked. Which means I should have chosen a different tape. John Lennon's massive ego was about to challenge me.

I could tell the class were restless as soon as the music started. The day before, everyone had been loudly singing along to '*Soo-pah-pah Troop-pah-pah*' and now I was asking them to sing along to '*Everybody talk about badism, shagism, dragism, madism....*' They didn't want to. Miss Ellsworthy tried to make me feel better by attempting to get everybody to join in with '*All we are saying is give peace a chance...*' but I could tell that nobody's hearts, except mine and hers, were in it. And then, during the tracks that followed, Miss Ellsworthy seemed to lose interest as well. I tried to explain to her. 'There are good Beatles records and bad Beatles records and you just have to accept that it's not all nice to listen to but it doesn't matter because they are geniuses.' She said, 'Is that right, Hayley?' and then, just as John Lennon started singing, *Woman is the Nigger of the World*, she said, 'I've heard enough now,' and pressed Stop.

And quite frankly, I was relieved, because clearly this song belonged so firmly in the naked and hairy and tuneless category that I didn't even have the energy to defend it. And right then and there, I wasn't actually sure how I felt about John Lennon and The Beatles anymore. Could such a rude song be excused by the brilliance of *Happy Xmas (War is Over)*? I wasn't sure. As I laboured, cheeks burning with shame, over my cross-stitch and looked wistfully out of the Quiet Room window to watch the boys fly their paper planes, the sophistication of John Lennon's words was completely lost on me. Yes, John Lennon had spoken to me. But what he appeared to be saying was, 'I am a dirty, dirty man'.

So I may have failed on that occasion to re-evaluate the position of women in society, but what I did learn that day was that my tastes in pop music as a nine-year-old girl were strangely out of kilter with all of my female peers and Miss Ellsworthy. Something about me was out of step.

Fast-Forward twenty-three years to a café in the centre of Cardiff. It's Saturday night. The café is crowded. Many of the people sat at the tables and propped up at the bar have come to hear me and my friend Kirsty play our special blend of Sixties funk, soul and beat records. The atmosphere is good and the venue is right. There is just one problem. We are on the wrong side of the record decks. The café has double-booked its DJs.

'Er... who are you?'

On the right side of the record decks, two men regard us scornfully before honouring us with a reply. 'Mad Soul. And this is our patch. We've been spinning the soul around here for months. Years even. You're not needed. Go home.'

Kirsty and I stand our ground. It's not about the loyalty we feel to our friends who have shown up to support us, nor is it about defiance of these two smug men who set up their equipment first. It's just that neither of us has a clue what to do next.

The man who has spoken gives a sigh and tries again. 'Look girls, it might be your little hobby, but this is our life. Playing records is our life. It's not a game or anything and we do this as professionals. So put your Greatest Hits records and your re-issues back in your car and leave it to the big boys, yeah?'

Even in the dim gloom of the café, I notice Kirsty's face flush and I lower my gaze and stare at my trainers. The man in front of me is neither big nor a boy. He is only a few inches taller than me and he looks far too old to be having such an altercation in a café. He looks older even than I am.

'Can't we do half a night each?'

The two dads behind the turntables shake their shoulders and share a derisive laugh.

'We've got our own punters to think about. They come here to hear something brilliant. We can't have people turning up on a Saturday night to listen to any old shit.'

'We're not going to play any old shit.'

The vocal dad leans over across the decks and glances

down contemptuously at the two silver record boxes resting by my and Kirsty's feet.

'What you got in there? Got any Betty Wright? Marlena Shaw? Terry Callier? I bet you ain't got any Terry Callier in there, have you?' There is a silence. Neither Kirsty or I have any idea who Terry Callier is. Dad senses this and stands back with a triumphant sneer. 'They've never bloody heard of Terry Callier! Girls, you might just as well go and throw all your records in the river if you've not got any Terry Callier in your box.'

Irritated, I manage to find my voice. 'Oh yeah? Well, I've got quite a lot of Stevie Wonder in my record box. I don't know if you've heard of him? And Diana Ross? She used to be in a band called The Supremes...?'

I stop talking because I can feel the red mist descending. I hang my head and look down at my trainers again.

Dad Soul collectively sigh noisily and decide that it will be easier to play the part of the indulgent patrons. 'OK, OK, girls, don't get your knickers in a twist. It's obviously that time of the month innit. How about you warm them up for the first ninety minutes and then we'll come back and play the rest. How does that sound?'

Kirsty and I nod our heads. Ninety minutes is better than no minutes.

Vocal Dad ushers us around to the other side of the decks. 'Now you do know how to use a record player, properly, don't you? Just stick with the cross-fader to mix. It's more simple. We're going to the pub next door for a bit. There's nothing you'll play that we won't have already heard. Now, stick to the cross-fader, remember. We don't want to come back and find anything broken.'

19

'Yeah, and no scratching,' his mate adds. 'As if they'd know how to!' The two of them laugh and head out of the café.

I somehow manage a smile of acquiescence and keep my mouth shut until they've both disappeared from sight. When the door closes, I allow myself one word of indulgence. 'Cock!'

'Wanker!'

'Dickhead!'

'Cu–.' Kirsty's final word on the matter is cut off by the jubilant opening chords of the Hammond organ on Aretha Franklin's *Rock Steady*. I am relieved because I don't think I would have been able to trump it.

But now that Aretha is playing, Dad Soul has ceased to matter anyway. That is the power and beauty of music. It is able to reach out and touch human emotion in a manner that no other art form is quite so effective at doing. Now that Aretha's voice is filling every corner of the café, I feel wonderful. I can feel the funky and low-down feeling that she is singing about. I feel happy.

Just before the track ends, Kirsty pulls out the Spencer Davis Group and blends Aretha's fading vocals into *I'm a Man* and we both bob up and down and yell out, '*I'm a man, yes I am and I can't help but love you so.*' The fact that neither of us are men does not matter in the slightest. The message of the lyric, when set to music, is so vibrant and overwhelming that while the record spins, I actually wish I were a man just so that I could go home and sing it to my wife.

The record ends and I give a cheery wave to my husband who is sat in a corner of the café with his friends. I can see nodding heads and re-filled glasses of beer. Everyone is enjoying themselves.

Stooping to return Aretha Franklin to the silver box, I pause for a second and admire the album sleeve. The artwork on the cover is as arresting as her vocal performance. Aretha is larger than life and devoid of any make-up but still she glows with a natural beauty that seems to shine out brightly through the depths of her brown eyes. She is dressed in a bright orange kaftan and her head is wrapped in a matching scarf. Behind her, there appears to be a stained-glass mosaic. The image is repeated four times, each from a slightly different perspective. She looks like a high African priestess who has come to preach her gospel to a world that waits. Waits to hear Aretha's truth. A truth as bare and blunt and triumphant as the album title which is printed in capital letters above the photograph.

'You guys are amazing! This music is amazing! I used to DJ a bit in Aberdeen. Have you got anything from *The Italian Job* soundtrack?'

I look up to see who has interrupted my thoughts. A woman, late twenties and Scottish accent, stands above me with a huge grin on her face. I smile back and pull out the record she has requested. An original copy, of course. Her grin gets even bigger. 'You know what, seeing you guys has made me think I might dig out my records again. This is brilliant!'

She gives a wave and then disappears off to the bar leaving me and Kirsty to get back on with it. The café is more crowded than ever. I notice with some relief that nobody seems to mind that it is us who are playing and not Dad Soul. A man, early twenties and Cardiff accent, passes us by on his way towards the loos and does a double-take. 'Two girls playing tunes. Cool!'

I grin. It is nice to be appreciated by a nice-looking young bloke even if I am ten years older than him and married. I look around the café for the man who is one year older than me and also married. To me. I catch his eye and give him an even bigger grin. Having his appreciation is better still. I turn back to the decks and lose myself for the millionth delicious time in the spiralling whirl of black vinyl.

We never saw Dad Soul again until closing time. Apparently, the lure of the cheap beer next door was too much for them and they took the professional decision to award themselves a night off. When they returned at the end of the night for their equipment, they were greeted by a happy café clientele and delighted bar staff who told them how well we had held the fort. We were granted a grudging respect. They said we had done well 'for a couple of birds'.

As I packed my records back into my box at the end of that evening, I found my mind suddenly hijacked by one of those blurred random memories which inexplicably work their way loose from the deeper recesses of my brain and snap into focus for seemingly no reason. For a split-second, I could see Miss Ellsworthy's tight-lipped, disapproving face again and the bewildered glances of the girls in the Quiet Room who wondered why I had chosen to bring in a John Lennon cassette rather than Showaddywaddy or Cliff Richard. And just at that moment, twenty-three years after first being baffled and embarrassed by John Lennon's words, I think, at last, I finally came to understand them.

But John Lennon was only partly right. *If* woman is the nigger of the world, then it's only because, sometimes, life is not always so easy. It may be harder to express yourself and you can often encounter prejudice along the way when you try.

But just because it's harder doesn't mean it can't be done and doesn't mean that the results can't be amazing. Sometimes, it's the struggle to be heard that makes it all worthwhile. John Lennon lamented the fact that women have to paint their faces, stay at home and lead a life of subjugation to men. But he was assuming that women are resigned to that. He was forgetting the small matter of an indomitable spirit.

That night, in the café, surrounded by people who were all having a great time because of the music that me and Kirsty were playing, we knew that we *weren't* the niggers of the world. Far from it. Just like Aretha Franklin had proudly proclaimed in capital letters to an audience of startled Sixties housewives and white record-buying men, we were young, gifted and black. And our souls were intact.

'Here Come the Hippie Niggers!'

Layla Jabero

This account is an edited version of an interview between the editor and Layla, conducted in 2005.

My first memory is of Glyneirw, the commune where I was born and where I lived with my English mother Tina and Iraqi father John, brother Ziad and about thirty other people. I was riding a tricycle and Ziad was riding a bike. We were going out to feed the chickens and we saw a wolf. I must have been three and he was six. I was frozen with fear and couldn't get off my tricycle so Ziad had to drag me off. We told everyone in the house that we'd seen a wolf but they just laughed at us. When they went out to the chickens later, half had been eaten. So we were like, 'Yeah, you didn't believe us, but it was true!'

I don't remember a lot from the really early days. We were in a big kids' room – there were at least ten of us. And there were more than twenty adults there. As kids, we just stuck together and did our own thing and all the adults stuck together and did theirs.

Glyneirw was a big manor house near Aberporth in what

is now Ceredigion. It had a walled garden where we used to play. It was a secret garden like you'd see in films. We used to explore everywhere and spent our time outside. In the summer we always ended up in the fields, especially the strawberry fields. My other favourite thing to do was to play in the bullocks' fields. John always says that when they started running towards me I thought they were coming to play with me. Everyone would say, 'Where's Layla?' Then they'd realise that I was probably in with the bullocks again and come looking for me.

I would often go a day without seeing anyone who was an authority figure. It felt as though we could do pretty much what we wanted. My brother Ziad was always injuring himself, falling out of trees and that. But it was quite nice that we weren't really told what to do, ever.

If I was being unkind, I guess I'd say the grownups were sitting around getting stoned. But they were also trying to make a living. The commune was supposed to be self-sufficient. There was a pottery there and some farming and a vegetable garden, and we made butter. Tina used to drive the tractor. She used to love driving the tractor and the trailer.

I don't know if being on a commune worked. It depends what the ideal of a commune should be. If it were to be 'peace, love and happiness' then I don't think it did. I remember there being so many arguments between people. And I think it was quite incestuous. Some people go to communes for 'free love' but I don't know.... My impression was that people couldn't live together too well. It was both too isolated and too intense.

Some people came for a couple of months then left and

that changed the balance because they didn't contribute so much. Some people were really committed and then some people wanted to drop out of their lives for a year. Of course there was friction between the workers and the freeloaders.

My parents met in London when John was a student. I've seen photos of him looking dapper in a sharp suit. Tina was five years younger. She went to a convent school but was expelled. After London, they lived in Bristol in a pretty hellish house with some serious drug addicts. Then Tina got pregnant and they decided they didn't want to bring Ziad up in that kind of environment, so I think they moved a couple of times then arrived at the commune in Wales.

A lot of people had flings with one another at Glyneirw – it was part of the culture. In 'normal' society it's such a big deal if that happens. In an ideal world, it would be great if you could be like that and people didn't get hurt by it all; it's not a bad way of looking at things. Tina hates any sort of institution; all of the crap that sometimes goes with being part of society and you can see why people would want to escape it and set up their own. You wonder, though, if it's ever possible to achieve.

There were fallings-out at the commune and when everything finally became too complicated, we left. After that, I went to the Montessori school. There was a feeling of things falling apart then and I hated it. Charlene, the main teacher there, used to want you to talk about your feelings all the time, but I was only four! I remember hating it. I used to sit around with tambourines and bang them. I was a bit of an arsehole and liked to be nasty to people – I don't know why. I got a load of rosehips and cut them up and put them down people's backs, as if to say, 'That's what I think of your emotions!'

Ziad got to go to a proper school because he was older. He got a lot of shit at Aberporth School for being the hippie kid, so he moved to the school in St Dogmael's where we were living for a while. One of the brothers next door and his mates were really awful to Ziad and used to be pretty aggressive. Sometimes they'd try to hurt me and so Ziad stuck up for me. So he'd get it instead. Ziad really used to cop it and we got to the point where we sometimes wouldn't play outside. The youngest brother, Judd, was the nicest and, weirdly, my younger sister Ella has a child with him now.

By the time Ella was born, we were living at Morfa. It was different there from the start. There were a lot of different families there so it was a bit like a commune. Hermes and Merlin and Jools lived there. They were wild kids and in that sense we were quite similar, so we did a lot together. Ziad was a bit wilder. I was just an idiot! I look back now and I'm so embarrassed and ashamed. I was just really angry. Tina always says people came to the house and would say, 'Hello Layla!' and I'd just say, 'Fuck off'. That was my catchphrase.

I don't think I was the happiest when I was growing up, even though it wasn't horrible. I tended not to get on with the other kids. Usually I'd fight them, as if to say, 'Get off my patch!'

I got on better with older boys, because I idolised Ziad. I didn't want to have anything to do with girls my age. I was a tomboy from the start. So we played football and climbed trees and played army.

We used to get called 'nigger' at school which, looking

back, was classic ignorance. Paki, blacky, nigger, they called us. At primary school, Blaenffos, the local kids used to shout, 'Here come the hippie niggers!' I used to want to have blonde hair and white skin and I'd say to John, 'It's all your fault! If you hadn't been from Iraq....' I was deadly serious. But, looking back now, it's ridiculous.

We learnt very quickly not to mention what went on at home. Little farming villages like Blaenffos were quite conservative. We used to get into a lot of fights. That was our way of dealing with it. If they called us names we'd just punch them. John was typically philosophical about the whole thing, calmly saying, 'Well, if they call you a name call it to them back!' So that's pretty much what we did.

The first year at Preseli (a small comprehensive secondary school in the hills) I got some shit but I basically beat anyone up who said anything bad to me. But Ziad was quite cool and he'd paved the way for me so it wasn't too bad. After about a year people stopped saying bad things to me. But I was in trouble all the time. If I just stood my ground sometimes that would be enough. But I didn't really care anyway. I just had that rage – when people said stuff I would just go mad. But I never wanted to be the one who said, 'Ooh they called me names,' and go and whimper about it. So that was my way of dealing with it. Ziad always told me off but he was exactly the same.

I was quite insecure about it all and about Morfa. Not because it was an awful place to be but just because I knew it was different to how other people lived. And some of those people then were my best friends. I'd go to their houses and not once would they come home to us – never. Because I didn't want them to see how we lived.

Tina would always be outside gardening naked. The moment it was sunny she'd strip off. We were used to it. I'd bring home friends that I thought were cool, and I'd be thinking, 'Please don't let Tina be outside gardening naked now!' There was such a cultural divide. And I never let John come to parents' evening. He wasn't allowed because he had a massive beard and an afro. I'd say to him, 'If you come I'll get teased forever'. It was so mean!

John being John – he's so lovely – he'd have wanted to get into it; to find out why I was feeling that emotion. He wouldn't take it personally. Which was just as well! I used to always say, 'Why can't we be normal!'

I used to try to get him to shave but he said it'd be a pain in the bum, 'If I started shaving, I'd have to do it all the time!' He felt the same way about cutting his hair. We were dreadful. We used to gang up on him. John was the one we were most embarrassed about. He just looked so wild. He looks totally respectable now.

This time last year John, Kai – Ella's son – and I went to the beach. Kai had this plastic sword with him and, at one point, I was at one end of the beach. John and Kai were walking along the rocks and John was carrying Kai's sword. I took a photo of him and he looks like something out of *Lord of the Rings* as he stumbles over the rocks, his massive hair blowing in the wind, waving his sword around.

It was only when I developed a good bond with my form teacher, who was also my Welsh teacher – Miss Williams – that I started to behave. I was a totally different person in my third and fourth years. I worked really hard and was a lot more ambitious. When I was in primary school I wanted to be an archaeologist. I remember telling my primary teacher how to spell it. But something happened between that and being taught by Miss Williams.

Miss Williams wrote something in my report at the end of Year Nine. My reports were usually so dire but she said the most positive thing I had ever read, 'If she stopped and thought for a minute and focused on her talents, she could be tremendously successful and could achieve a lot.' I took it home and I thought about it hard over the summer holidays. After that I completely changed. And that's when I decided I wanted to be a teacher. I was just so grateful to her because she tried to see the best in me. She taught me Welsh A-level. I'm fluent in Welsh because of her. She appreciated me, so I listened. She had a massive influence on everything I've done since then. I started to make more Welsh friends and I could understand what was going on when I went round their houses. I felt a part of it.

Around this time, I began to mellow a little and get to know people in the village and so many different people at school. There were some lovely people in Blaenffos and at school – for instance, many of them had encouraged me to go to the eisteddfod to compete in singing or *cyd-adrodd*[1] in Welsh. Lots of them would stop and talk to me and I loved trying out my Welsh with them and I think they really appreciated the fact that I was so keen to learn Welsh. I was certainly coming to recognise that there were many more positive forces around me than some of the negative taunts I had experienced in the past.

When I was in my early teens I tried drugs, like all the

other hippie kids, but it didn't feel quite right. In that respect, Ziad was different. 'The more naughty the better' was Ziad's approach. So it was one area where I wasn't influenced by him. Something from within stopped me. As time went on I started to think that sport was better. Better for you and you enjoy it. And people were telling me I was good at it. I started out playing hockey (county and regional), and loved playing all sports, especially football. And I got drawn to people like that – sporty people. I never talked to them about the stuff I did at the weekend. I thought they'd disapprove of it all. In the end, I had a big choice to make and I chose sport. Since then, sport has been a massive focus for me, especially football. I also think it probably keeps me out of trouble!

I always used to play football with the boys in the schoolyard. Six or seven of us girls got Mike Davies, the geography teacher, to do a football session with us a lunchtime a week. He didn't really see the point because we weren't going to play any matches. But all we wanted was to get better at football and play it. We begged and begged until we wore him down. He was really committed then. During the summer tournament he coached us in his own time. And when we entered the Newcastle Emlyn five-a-side tournament we won two years running.

At fifteen or sixteen I couldn't play in goal any more because I was too short. So I started playing outfield. I joined Newcastle Emlyn ladies team who were a fantastic group of people. I was the youngest so they all used to look after me. A lot of Welsh was spoken in the changing rooms and on the pitch. They used to call me Giggsy and I wore the number 11 shirt. I felt like I really fitted in.

From fifteen I was adamant I was going to Loughborough

University. This mainly came from John who, when I said I wanted to be a PE teacher, told me I should go to Loughborough. I'd never even heard of the place. I wanted to put down just one university on my UCAS form. I said I'd stay and re-sit until I got to Loughborough.

I am really short; I read Bryan Robson's autobiography which said he was too. The way he dealt with it was to drink Guinness and raw egg in the morning – it couldn't make him taller but it could make him stronger. So I started doing that. Tina and John bought me Guinness in the weekly shop when I was about fifteen, so I used to have the same as Bryan Robson every morning before school. The egg made the Guinness more bearable. None of it worked though!

After Loughborough University, I moved to Southampton to play in the Premier League. But about three weeks after joining Saints I broke my leg at the school where I'd just started teaching. I'd fallen awkwardly and it was a bad break, so I was off school for nine weeks. I couldn't play football for a year and I couldn't teach. It was quite a lonely time.

The following season was really awful. I was unfit and lacking in confidence. They weren't seeing the best in me and I was getting really depressed because football is so important to me. Week after week I was on the bench or I was dropped and in the end I couldn't be bothered to work on my fitness because it wasn't getting me anywhere.

I decided to have one last go. So I tried Brighton, which was in the same league. And if I couldn't get in there I'd drop down a league to below national premier. Luckily that went well. I really worked hard for it. I stayed at Brighton for three seasons and have just moved to Reading Royals LFC who are in the same league.

I love the togetherness of a team sport, the sense of community. Little things like that have always mattered to me, like our football team all wearing the same shirts in the bar in Loughborough having a sing-off against another team. Or even to the point of all of us in the PE department I lead wearing the same polo shirts to work.

My ambition is still the same – to play for Wales in a European Championship or World Cup. If I really focused on it I think I could. But work is drawing me away. You've got to sustain the training to be fit enough at that level. It's all about fitness and I am too into my work to put the hours in and perhaps now the opportunities have passed me by.

Wales are not as good as England but no matter how good I was it would never have been my dream to play for England. Pulling on a Welsh shirt and singing the national anthem means so much. However hard a time you've had in the place you grew up, and however ambivalent you might feel about it now, it is still home, and still somewhere that defines who you are and how you are.

I suppose that's why it's been tough for John since Iraq has been under attack from the West. I remember the night that war was announced in 1991. We stayed up really late and watched the first bombings. John was poker-faced. It was difficult to know what he was thinking. He'd cut himself off from Iraq and felt like he couldn't go back; didn't want to, and didn't have much to do with his family. But at the same time he really did care about it. Especially since his family was in Baghdad. His parents moved to Basra to get away because they thought it would be safer.

Since the recent war, John's got in touch with his family. He phones them up a lot more, which is really unusual. He talks about it more now, maybe because we ask him more about it. I didn't want him to be Iraqi/Caldenian before but now I appreciate it as part of me.

I think it's a good thing to have got Saddam Hussein out. It's easier now. When we used to talk to our family in Iraq, John would tell us to be careful about what we said as everything was echoed back because they were tapping the phone. Now you can talk openly. They send emails now, too, which they couldn't have done before. I've been sent photos by email so I've seen what my grandmother, aunt and cousins look like. That was so lovely.

Now I think one day I might be able to go there and I never thought that before. I'd love to go. John just says to 'be careful'. When they invaded Kuwait I felt really uncomfortable. I was worried about what people would think. People would say to me, 'Jabero's a lovely name. Where's that from?' and I used to say, 'It's Arabic.' I never said it was from Iraq – I was so worried about it. My best friend said, 'Why don't you just say Iraq? You should be proud of it.' Ever since then I say I'm half Iraqi, and I am proud of it. Some people say, 'We're at war with you.' Adults say that to me! That's when I realise I've matured because I wouldn't punch them now.

I've become much more aware as I've got older. When the Iraq war started I watched News 24 all the time. Mostly it was just because I was worried about my family. But also I felt that I had some part in it. That I had some sort of link with the people in Iraq. It's still shit out there – a total mess. And my family are quite scared. They're Christian and for Christians it's a scary time because a lot of the churches have been bombed. But I think they're pleased to have Saddam out. I feel strongly about them being my family even though I've never met them. You just hope that they can rebuild the country. Selfishly, I hope that it happens in my lifetime so I can go there.

My life now seems a million miles away from a commune. It is quite rigid and I feel constantly busy. I have to play football. I have to train. I have to see my friends. And then, what's left? It works for me. But I imagine other people look in and think, 'Why can't you find a nice man and settle down?'

It's not the rule to settle down and have kids, and seeing as I have conformed in every other aspect of my life, maybe I should be a little different. Then sometimes that conformist streak returns and I start setting silly targets like being married with two children in five years' time!

I don't think of Southampton as my home. I don't know where home is, really I don't. I used to think it was Loughborough. I think I'm passionately Welsh. But I can't see myself living in Wales. Yet. When I think of Wales I think of the quietness and the distance from everything and everyone and I can't see myself living like that. But then there's something about it, how beautiful it is, my feelings for the place. You do stop when you go home. Everything stops. You forget the world you've left is still going on.

Notes

[1] Cyd-adrodd – group recital

From This Day Forth

Holly Howitt

I am five, and have just started primary school. I am sitting in the canteen, which also morphs into the gym and the assembly hall. I am precariously balanced on a burgundy plastic seat, looking at the sad collection of vegetables and some kind of meat on my plate, and wanting my mum's spaghetti bolognaise instead. The canteen smells slightly rancid, and I miss the smell of patchouli in my own home. I am young for my year, and although I've been coming to nursery here for nearly a birthday's worth of months, I am uncomfortable, because I don't feel ready. Earlier today, I drew a picture of a unicorn. Mrs Williams kindly asked, 'What's that? Is it for me?'

'No,' I said. 'It's for my mummy.'

Now, I am sitting opposite a girl I already know as belligerent and unkind. In nursery she always wanted to be Queen Infant, stealing the spades so no one else could play in the sandpit, and eating all the cress we were growing for salad sandwiches before we had a chance. She is called Talia, and she's bigger than me with a very loud voice.

'Holly, Holly, Holly,' she chants, for no real reason except she knows I'm frightened of her and she can stare at me. She is a large child, wearing a pleated grey skirt rather than the grey pinafores infants' parents favour, possibly because they don't make pinafores for big girls like her. She has lots of black hair, a constant scowl, and broad shoulders. The worst thing about Talia is that she is the oldest in the year, and because of this, has an air of knowing everything. She looks me straight in the eye and I look down at my plate, which is chipped. Jenny, who is sitting next to me, looks like she will burst into tears. I assume that this is simply due to Talia's presence.

'Leave Holly alone and eat your food, Talia,' says Mrs Williams, who is supervising our ham-fisted attempts to use the school's rather large and tarnished cutlery.

'Can I go to the toilet?' Talia asks.

'No, you must wait till after your dinner.'

'But Miss...'

'No, Talia, do what you're told.'

Talia looks around for something or someone to worry.

'Holly, I'm going to be an actress when I grow up. I am, I am. Holly, do you want to get married?' Talia asks.

'No,' I say, though I'm not sure why.

'Haha, you have to, it's the law!'

'No it isn't,' I say, and it feels like that's the right answer. My mum's married, and my friends' mums are married, but I am sure that what she says can't be true. I think about my role models, searching for the truth. She-Ra isn't married. But Bow is chasing after her, I know that. I have the doll version of Bow and you can make his heart beat when She-Ra comes near by pushing in a little button at his spine. Who else is there? The women in *Dynasty* aren't all married, I'm sure, and they look pretty grown up to me. My Gran. She's not married. Hmm.

'Yes it is, if you're a lady you have to get married, it's the law,' she says, and I see her fists slam on the table. 'You have to, when you're grown up.'

'No, that's not true.'

'It's the law, it's the law, it's the law...'

'No it isn't!'

'It is, it is, it is, you have to even if you don't want to!'

I feel a hot stream of tears down my face. It's not because I know I'm right. It's that I'm terrified that I'm wrong. Instead of asking the best question, which would be how on earth she knows any of that, or instead of smugly ignoring her in disbelief, I just feel terror flush my face and make my palms sweat. My fork slips out of my hand, but lands flat and silent on the table. At that moment I realise that I don't want to be owned, and certainly not by a big man who will steal my surname. It is the stuff of nightmares.

'But I don't want to.'

'Haha,' she laughs, simply.

I run away from the table, pushing back my plastic chair, to Mrs Pritchard the dinner lady, who is supervising the older children putting their slops from finished meals into a bucket. She wheels round as I tug at her skirt. She looks very cross, her lips pursed like shrivelled raisins. I sob into her skirts, and they smell like the summer holiday just gone.

Holly Howitt

'Mrs Pritchard, Talia says it's the law, she says that you have to get married when you grow up, she says that all girls have to get married.' My voice is broken with sobs, and I think of all the wedding pictures I've ever seen – my mum's, my cousin's and my aunt's, and think that they all must have been pretending to smile. I look up into Mrs Pritchard's face, but she's smiling.

'It's not the law, love. You don't have to if you don't want to. But you will, one day. Have you finished your dinner? Where's your plate?'

I often think back to that incident and wonder what on earth made me cry. It could have been just because I was frightened of Talia (which seemed like a clairvoyant intuition as she ended up being taken into care after a violent mental breakdown at the age of nineteen). It could have been because I hated being wrong. (A very strong possibility – I was a stubborn and rather obnoxious child when I was armed with information; my parents would all but weep with frustration when I stomped around singing my favourite refrain: 'I'm right, I'm right, I'm right.') But when I think hard, I start to wonder whether it was some kind of fear of the unknown, some kind of horror of being someone else's rather than my own.

When I was fourteen, my older sister asked what I would do if someone told me they loved me. I imagine she only asked out of some kind of need for advice in her 'complicated' life of teenage angst. But I thought about it seriously, and my answer was instantaneous.

'I'd be sick, and tell them to piss off,' I said.

'What about if they wanted to get married?' she asked.

'I'd run away.' Where that certainty came from I'm not sure – but I know that I was probably right to believe it.

'I don't believe in vegetarians,' Kayleigh said.

'They're not like fairies; it's not a question of belief,' I replied, knowing both that no one else was listening, nor would they bother to take the meaning from what I'd said if they had.

'Yeah, but I think it's stupid,' she said, thus confirming that she hadn't got a clue, either of what I said or what it meant.

The conversation began to dry up, but that had little to do with me. It was simply because she had stopped talking.

By the end of that week, I knew that I had to leave that office. It wasn't really the people, the job or the pay, but more a combination of everything eventually forming itself into a simmering repression that threatened to boil over on several frightening occasions. I'm not the most tolerant of people anyway – I get pissed off very quickly in queues, even inevitable ones, and anyone who pushes in front of me to the press of drunkards lining a bar should watch their backs – but I really did try my best. It was just that everything seemed to be under constant scrutiny, and the results of this examination always ended in some tactless (though, in their eyes, honest) comment. The way I spoke ('you're not Welsh'), the things I ate, and even the way I dressed were discussed openly. Once, one of the girls in the office stopped talking to me for a whole day because the skirt I was wearing made her 'depressed'. But it just seemed so barmy that I laughed, I made the tea, I did jobs that really weren't for me to do. My patience was wearing thin as the months stretched on. And on. In some ways, I relished the way that nobody listened to a word I said, but at the same time I resented it. If they did listen to me, my words were met with incredulity. What, you don't have milk in your coffee? What, you're scared of driving? What, you're tired? Why? You don't do anything here! What must you get up to at night... ad nauseam, the same jokes always at my expense. At times, I found it funny, and the people who made the jokes always meant well. But what I did mind was that there was no fluidity in the thoughts, no questioning of the concrete ideas that had festered throughout all their years trapped in the sweltering office. And the way that in this murk, tactlessness thrived.

The biggest problem about me for them was something unimportant to me: that somehow I wasn't meshing neatly with their ideas of womanhood. It was the question of 'settling down' (gah – even the phrase sends shivers down my spine). Not one person could believe that I didn't want a joint mortgage, I didn't want to get married, and, worst of all, I do not want children. At Christmas time, I was asked what my boyfriend was buying me as my present. I replied that I didn't know, which was true – I like surprises, I said. And they smirked and winked and looked at each other, and I didn't know why. 'It's an engagement ring,' they said. And do you know what? It wasn't. And do you know what's worse? I was actually disappointed when I didn't get one. Disappointed? What, I hear you cry? It was exactly what I didn't want! I'm only twenty-two! I'm not sure about anything apart from my own uncertainty! Marriage would make me run away! I worried that I was starting to believe their propaganda. After years of forthright though rather naïve attempts to be a feminist, I wondered if I really was starting to become the woman Mrs Pritchard warned me of – the one who would want to, one day.

Even though I worked at that office for less than a year, I took a lot of days off sick. They weren't faked though. The bad air-conditioning and the dirty kitchen made the office a haven for pestilence and plague. People with heavy colds seemed to like using my phone as their own, and their noses dribbled into it, their sneezes caked it, and some people even left their snotty tissues behind on my seat when they were finished. I often had stomach bugs, and once I had one that spiralled through the whole weekend. I dragged myself to work on Monday, even though it was freezing and I felt pretty rancid, knowing what they'd all be saying about my absence on Friday.

'Good weekend?' Kayleigh asked, perched at her desk with a fresh, steaming cup of coffee in her hand. I noted that there was not one on my desk.

'No, I spent most of it being sick,' I said, sitting down and realising there were more people milling about in the office than I'd first thought.

'Ooh, did you feel sick in the morning?' asked Heather, my boss.

'I felt sick all the time,' I said, trying to avoid further comment. Looks were exchanged, and smirks badly hidden.

'Not morning sickness then...'

'No. Not at all,' I said indifferently.

'Well, you'd better get your skates on anyway,' said Hywel, who I worked fairly closely with. 'You haven't got long left if you want to have kiddies.'

There were so many things I could have said at this point. So many I nearly screamed them all at once. *What do you think I am, some fucking time bomb of fecundity? A walking womb waiting to be widened?* Or, I could have made the point, *I'm twenty-two, not fifty-two, and maybe you don't understand women as well as you think.* Or, I could have just said what I was burning to say, the word that had already formed on the top of my throat – *cunt*. Instead, I did what I had learnt to do – remain silent, smile, and keep my fists under the table.

I thought about when I first met Hywel. It was my first week, and it was autumn. Everyone had colds. Hywel had a particularly bad one, and as he walked past me, he sneezed very forcefully into his hands. I pulled a face which unfortunately he spied. He walked over and wiped his snotty hands all over my back. And what did I do? I did nothing. I just sat there and shuddered, feeling so small I thought I'd cry – just like when I sat by Talia. *You dirty, fat, stinking shit,* I wanted to say. *You complete and utter arsehole. I wouldn't touch your hand if I were slipping into a fiery abyss and you were my only chance of rescue.* But I just sat there, like a complete twat, thinking over and over how much I hated my life. Pathetic.

I was ashamed of my job as a secretary. After two degrees, I really had no idea what I wanted to do next, but I knew I needed some money. My flat was mouldy, but I still had to pay for the privilege of living there. I had written a novel but I was pretty sure that no one would want it. All my friends had left Cardiff, and I wasn't sure about going on to do a PhD. So I scoured the papers and saw that being a secretary was simply my best bet. But as soon as I'd started there, I pretended that it wasn't really me, that it wasn't really my real job, oh no. I had plans. It was a stop-gap, I just needed the money. But by acting the way I did I belittled myself more. When I went out one weekend, I got chatting to a young man at the bar. He was dressed casually and had messy hair. He offered to buy me a drink. I refused. He carried on chatting.

'So, what do you do?' he asked, innocuously. I was too drunk to lie.

'I'm a secretary,' I said, thinking, *He's going to think you're thick now; that you're going nowhere*.

'Cool! Do you wear those sexy glasses and a tight skirt to work?'

'Er,' I edged away, feeling both flattered and disgusted at the same time. It was the sort of question I got all the time from men, along with, 'Was I my "boss's bit of fluff"?' When I told them she was female, they had eyes like saucers.

I shouldn't have cared what anyone thought about me, least of all predictable men at bars, and I shouldn't have fallen into the trap of equating work with worth. *It doesn't matter. It's just money*. I shouldn't have cared what drunken men wanted to believe, just like I shouldn't have cared what my colleagues thought of my opinions, or what Mrs Pritchard had warned me of. But it's hard not to, when you're doing a job you hate and you have little else to think about. When your life becomes so static that you start to enjoy the ordinary. It makes me sound pretentious, or precious, or like I deserve some sort of privilege. It's not that. I just felt like I was turning into a woman whose life would never change. When I learnt that the only scope for long-term leave was maternity, it made me feel like a battery hen, my life already marked out by a system I didn't devise. I was so bitter that I burnt myself out with bad dreams, nightmares about staying in the job forever, being my boss' sidekick, squirrelled away with her secret paperwork about all our colleagues until she passed away in her chair, her body buried in the filing cabinet. There were dreams where I lived inside the photocopier, only occasionally seeing life through the glass when someone lifted the lid, dreams where I got pregnant with a mutant baby made out of paperclips and Pritt Stick, and I carried it close, filling out my form for long-term leave so I could escape the office. It made me feel like I was going mad, made me forgetful at work and prone to hot flushes throughout the day. Marriage was the last thing on my mind. The first was how to get out.

If I were to analyse these fears, I can see that they have something to do with ownership and uncertainty. That's all. But I like my surname, I like having my own bank account, and I like having an empty womb. When I decided to leave work, I told Heather that I was applying for a PhD, and if I got it, I would go within a month. She tried to blackmail me in an all too wifely way.

'What about financial security? Have you thought of that? What about you and your boyfriend? You can't stay in your flat forever, and what about getting married? If you stay here, I can offer you a promotion, stability.'

I don't know what I said, but inside the death was already complete. I had recognised something: I didn't want to be static, the only changes in my life implemented by a man. I didn't want anyone else's surname, and I wasn't interested in conception. I wanted to pick what I did, go somewhere where you were allowed to choose, and to be somewhere where the answer to anything wasn't 'One day you'll change your mind'. Well, maybe I will, but that's an option for me, not for anyone else. The choices we thought we had aren't so easy to take; there are boundaries everywhere which people would think you a fool to cross.

But in other ways it's liberating to realise that there really are choices, that you can actually see over the fences someone else has used to pen you in. I don't want to deny myself choice: I just want to view all of them first.

Some girls say that they've been dreaming about their wedding since childhood. Whenever I've dreamt about mine, there hasn't been a groom. There's just been me, my family and my friends, sunshine and beautiful flowers. It's more like a garden party than a wedding, and no one seems to care that my new owner isn't there.

2

Equally Cursed and Blessed

Bit on the Side

Robyn ap Gwilym

Yesterday my married lover asked me if I was a feminist. At the time, I didn't do myself – my beliefs – justice. For me, feminism is a given. Who could possibly argue with the idea that women and men should be paid the same wage for doing the same work? That sexual and domestic violence is abhorrent? That equal opportunities are not a luxury, but a right. This is the tactic I sometimes use on my undergraduate students, now that feminism seems to be a dirty word, associated as it is (apparently) with bitter spinsters and hairy lesbians, two cartoon characters I have never had the good fortune to come across in 'real' life.

I am a university lecturer, teaching 'new' degrees at a 'new' university, and last week, as we discussed the relative merits of *Sex and the City* the novel and *Sex and the City* the Channel 4 TV series against a backdrop of largely post-feminist theory, I found myself faced with the views of a bleach-blonde feisty Russian student suggesting that it was somehow irresponsible to transmit these images of thirty-something women as sexual predators.

Instinctively and intellectually disagreeing, I did what I always do in such pedagogically difficult moments. I said, 'What does everyone else think?' Should I tell my students that I am a bisexual spinster? That I had a threesome in Paris a couple of months ago? That the older I get the more I like to fuck? Of course I said nothing of the sort and other students explored their own embedded views on sexuality and gender through the characters encountered in the relatively safe haven of fiction.

My lover seemed to be suggesting that having an affair with him could be seen as some kind of slight (by me) of his wife (another woman). He was, of course, referring to a notion of 'sisterhood' that has more to do with the second wave of feminism, that of the Sixties and Seventies. The implication was that I am distancing myself from commitment to that tradition of social responsibility which sacrifices self and pleasure for the benefit of a greater cause (a role that wives, mothers and housewives know all too well). But at the time, I couldn't explain why – or didn't want to. Feminism may be a dirty word but post-feminism is an ugly hybrid.

Sometimes being a good feminist (first, second or third wave) is a struggle. Because being a woman often involves apologising for being *too much*. I have been told that I am too supportive, too responsible, too sensitive, too maternal, too bossy, too neurotic, too involved, too ambitious, too honest, too demanding – even that I love too much! It is not hard to see that the 'positive' criticisms are the flipside to the negatives. Responsible means involved; sensitive means neurotic; bossy means ambitious.

None of the attributes or faults listed may be diametrically opposed but our strengths are often our faults too. I'm not trying to wriggle out of any of the above; all of them may be true at some point: like most people, I have more than one self. But I am resisting a trend to label strong women as difficult. Despite my faults, I hope that I am a strong woman.

I was quite hung-over when the topic of feminism came up and was therefore not at my most lucid or persuasive. I had been out dancing, a little precariously at times, in my four-inch heels and skinny Guess jeans until 3am the night before. My feet still hurt and I didn't want to have to justify myself in front of someone whose quick-fire intellect intimidated me and whose presence in my life signalled an ambivalence that was, as yet, unresolved.

Quite rightly, you will already have your hand up, waiting to tell me that his betrayal is the greater – it is he who comes to visit his attractive younger lover on a sunny Saturday afternoon, briefcase in hand, as though he were headed for his Bloomsbury office. His question sidelined the greater dilemma of his own betrayal. But that is a given – unless you subscribe to a notion of blame in which it is the 'other woman' – the scarlet woman – who must be marked with a scarlet letter for her sin.

So now, sitting (singly) in the double bed of my still-new flat on a Sunday morning in Camberwell I am going to piece together my reasons for stating that I am some sort of a feminist. And maybe this will make or break the thin connective thread that attaches me to someone like him.

1. Compromise

How many of us got what we hoped for? The Christmas present from a parent that shows a worrying lack of taste but must be received with a smile through gritted teeth? The perfect job that leaves no time for a life? The man of your dreams who comes in around two minutes? The lover who promises to leave his wife for you but – surprise! – doesn't? A harmonious life of nights spent watching TV with a partner you look at with barely concealed contempt but are too afraid to leave? Welcome to the world of the post-feminist woman. The woman who can have it all but only wants 2.4 kids and a house with a garden. Or still doesn't know what it is she is looking for.

I know this one couple who are blissfully happy together – *this one couple*. Most of the rest are doing alright. When I look at what they have, I don't ever think, 'I wish I had what you have: him.' I see a beautiful blonde friend, a working mother, who is frustrated because her husband doesn't want to socialise or entertain any more and who tells me that when she walked up the escalators at Covent Garden tube the other day a stunning black man turned to her and said, 'You're really fit.' She thought that he meant that she exercised frequently, having learnt to forget her own vivacious magnetism. I have another friend who has been compulsively online dating for two years and has finally found someone sweet, bright, good-looking and solvent. But doesn't think she can fall for him completely. She has never fallen for anyone completely. What is this fairytale that these high-achieving gorgeous women subscribe to?

I have a lover who I see once or twice a week. If I didn't know that he was returning to his wife and family in Notting

Hill when he left my front door I think this would be the perfect relationship. Passion, banter and affection. And then a return to my interests, friends and independence. Who is it that is compromising the most here?

2. Guilt

There is a notion in feminist constructivist thinking that women have historically been 'split' – they view themselves as subject and object, because they are accustomed to being objectified by the male gaze or, more accurately, the patriarchal gaze. One of their only forms of control over themselves (particularly when women were predominantly domestic creatures) was over the body. The body is the site of objectification, reproduction and a site of power and control for women. But the body is also about sex and consumption and desire – drives that have historically been deemed too powerful for the gentler sex in the West and are therefore closely aligned with a sense of guilt about pleasure. The second sex comes second or not at all.

My only guilt about my lover is for myself: am I conning myself out of something more substantial? Something that would make me less vexed about a pattern I have fallen into, less concerned about my position in a society that 'views single women our age as sad', as Miranda, in *Sex and the City* puts it? Or do I feel guilty about not reproducing; about stealing another's man; about depriving his children of his time through my (selfish!) claim on his attention?

3. Nurture

Yesterday my lover was hungry. I never make him food – I save that intimacy for friends who can indulge and relax over a long lunch or dinner, not for the one with whom moments are snatched. We seldom eat together; the intensity of our meetings makes food seem trivial – a waste of time that could be spent locked into one another.

I made him cheese on toast though, yesterday. And bathed him after we made love. And kissed him a dozen times when he looked sad. And told him that his month away would be a good thing – a time in which to escape from his swathe of work and other commitments. Of course I didn't include myself in that (I didn't want to be a burden). Why didn't I want to be a burden? Because that would make me unattractive – a less appealing mistress.

However much I try to wriggle out of the expectations of my sex I find a slippage – a sense in which I know I can help the other (primary) person to feel better. If I sacrifice my needs enough, an impossible love will become possible.

Of course this is all bullshit.

4. Pleasure/Desire

I recently went on the hen weekend of a dear friend, whose other friends, generally, I'm less enamoured with. Among the group were four mothers, two mothers-to-be, three brides-to-be and lots of married women.

I am single. As it transpired, I was the only single woman there. I felt like an interloper. Or as if I was suffering from a terminal illness that nobody quite wanted to mention.

A hen weekend conjures images of reckless women wearing very little apart from L-plates, storming through some unsuspecting town's insalubrious bars and playing spin the bottle to outdo each other with filthy sexual secrets. You know, like when you gave your first blow job outside the school disco and were sick on his cock (no, you can't remember his name). Or when you finally made out with your best friend or enjoyed your first three-way. I realised when at 8pm on Friday evening not a drop of liquor had passed our lips, so intent were we on blowing up hen weekend balloons and preparing delicious food, that it probably wasn't going to be that sort of weekend. After breaking open a bottle, I learnt that I was also the only smoker – even though only an occasional and very considerate one – a vice for which I was quickly chastised by a woman I later learnt likes her husband to cut her toenails for her.

So I sensed somehow that regaling the group with tales of my last drug-fuelled conquest (a nineteen-year-old blond surf-god) which functioned as a useful distraction from the break-up with a former lover (an all-but-married colleague with a two-year-old child), wouldn't be quite the thing. Imagine the horror. Harlot! Child molester! Lock up your husbands! So my story was boiled down to one word: 'single'.

Even that, though, precipitated ripples of discomfort among the cushioned women on the sofas of the luxuriously nouveau riche lounge overlooking the sea. 'Oh,' was followed a few moments later by, 'I know someone single for you!' Perfectly sweet but a bit, you know, presumptuous. Perhaps I like being single. Or have no sex drive. Or don't like men. Or like women. Would any of those positions be so hard to swallow? (Clue: only one of them.)

And what if I'd spoken my mind in response to some of their more conventional wisdom? Or said, 'Married? God, you've got to sleep with the same man for the rest of your life? Poor you.' Or, 'So you're a stay at home mum then? Good job you chose a man who earns lots of money to support you rather than some creative intellectual type.' Or what if I'd said what I really think: that marriage is a form of prostitution; that weddings are a ridiculous but highly lucrative capitalist enterprise; that having children doesn't have to mean giving up on sex and drugs and rock and roll. I wonder....

I don't need a lover to fix my shelves, change my tyres, reign me in; protect me. I can pay someone to do the DIY – I have other skills and interests. I have a friend who helps me sort out my finances, another who sets up my broadband wireless and another (ex-lover – he did nothing practical while we were together) who is an artist and carpenter – I write press releases for his shows and he puts up my curtain rails and fixes my shed. I have a baby sister who I mother, and a mother whose passion for life is a constant inspiration to me.

What need do I have for a partner? Well, the things I sometimes crave are intimacy, sex and play. Guilt, compromise and pain I don't. And yet... it isn't so easy to shrug off the uniform of my gender and I too feel the need for pointless squabbles, nights in front of the TV, companionship, children. Sometimes, though, I don't know what's coming from me and what's been pre-set on my remote control.

5. Choice

I can choose to work or stay at home, have kids or not (by taking the pill or aborting), sleep with whom I want (providing consent is given) and spend my money on what I want. There is nothing particularly controversial about any of this for someone like me – educated, middle-class and supported by a network of friends and family.

But what about my affair? Did I choose it? Did I choose not to be married with children and a husband and a rose garden? Is this a form of self-flagellation or rather a reward?

I am someone who has always been in and out of love, who is accustomed to being wanted; the school cheerleader type. I know my charms but it may be that I am addicted to a certain sort of thrill. It may be that coming from a family repeatedly reinvented, broken and extended makes laughable the notion of merely 'you and I'. But I too have loved sweet men for years at a time – been in what might be termed 'good relationships'. These explanations are not enough.

I do want children. And although I can't imagine being with someone forever, neither do I savour the idea of bringing up kids on my own. Sometimes I wonder how it is that I've reached the age of thirty-two (and slept with as many men) but have never accidentally become pregnant.

I also wonder why some idiotic part of me has such a voracious appetite for fiction. You see, my lover tells me that he wants to have my children and we talk wistfully about how beautiful they would be. And then he leaves.

6. Pleasure/Pain

This is what my pain feels like. It feels like the sound of my father's voice thick with drink, calling me a bitch, on an otherwise pleasant Sunday afternoon. Telling me that 'I am not his family' because I ask him, very firmly, to call me back when he is sober, or not at all. We are no longer in contact. It is the man of my dreams rejecting me for being 'too much': too demanding; too emotional. For running off with my best friend. It is the disappointment in myself for not being what I don't believe in being (a success in terms of a currency I try not to use); for not having achieved what I could and should have; for sometimes feeling inadequate, angry, wounded; for being disappointed and ungrateful, occasionally, when I have so much.

My pleasure is less contrived, though. It can be found in a multitude of unexpected places: in the hard autumn sunlight in my very own home that makes me squint as I write; in an unknown new neighbour singing smiling greetings as he cycles under my roof terrace on a Saturday morning; in the long slow kisses of my fleeting darling; in the hugs of my little sister; in swimming in the sea in Pembrokeshire in summertime and walking along its coastline, my mind and body at one and free; in the feeling of hugging my best friend, who is swollen like an outsize water-melon the day before she is induced. In my lover making me address a question that I feared I might answer wrongly, but have not.

Before the Rain

Jo Mazelis

Sitting in Swansea's reference library, with its domed ceiling and cast-iron mezzanine upper levels, and looking through back issues of the local paper, the *Evening Post*, I found it was tempting to consider that time had barely changed anything and that the events of thirty years ago seemed as vivid and alive as ever.

The news story I was researching concerned a number of murders that had happened in the local area in the early Seventies. Murders that had been committed two years before the Yorkshire Ripper claimed his first victim in 1975, and long before Fred and Rosemary West's crimes were discovered. Murders that were committed even before the term *serial killer* was coined. Murders that had remained unsolved until the new millennium, and had all but passed the notice of the national press, and seemed also to have been all but forgotten locally, at least as far as the newspapers were concerned. Yet the feeling lingers that it is wrong for such crimes to slip out of sight and out of mind; wrong and indeed dangerous to forget that the killer or killers might still be walking free, and unforgivable that those girls whose lives were snatched from them so violently should be forgotten.

When I was seventeen, my friend and I had a routine. On Saturday mornings we worked together at the Spar supermarket in the Uplands. We stood at the lower end of the till and packed bags, and wore regulation uniform of pine-green zip-up overalls. I would daydream while I put tins of beans and peas and loaves of bread and hunks of meat into brown paper sacks or empty boxes. These daydreams were invariably about falling in love, though it was the sort of transforming love that thoroughly absorbed one, transported the self away from the dreariness of everyday life.

Just before the store closed at one, it was our job to help clean up and so we filled galvanised metal buckets with hot water and a mixture of Flash and bleach, and then mopped the aisles. After that we each collected our wage of one pound. We'd pop back to Debra's house, cook ourselves something appalling for lunch – we had a passion for Yeoman's instant mash to which we'd add a great deal of butter so that it turned yellow and greasy – then we'd change our clothes and go into the centre of Swansea to shop.

We scoured the stores for clothes, trying on skirts, tops, shoes, jewellery and jackets in Top Shop, Chelsea Girl, C & A, Etam and Dolcis. We had little money; even with our wages and pocket money and the extra cash nagged and cajoled out of a parent, we might each only have enough for a new hair accessory or jewellery or tights. We were continually attempting to reinvent ourselves, certain that if only we could obtain *that* baby doll dress, *those* knee-high platform boots, *that* long flowered gypsy dress we would somehow become perfect and desirable, and thus find love.

After town we'd go back to Debra's to bathe and get ready. We strived for beauty. We wanted to be noticed. We wanted a boy to catch sight of us across the crowded dance floor, for him to be drawn to us inexorably, unwillingly, and helplessly. Love at first sight was what we wanted. Happy ever afters.

On the night of September 15th 1973 we went, as had become our routine, to the Top Rank Suite on the Kingsway, Swansea. The Top Rank ballroom was part of a new complex that included the large single-screen Odeon and some retail units all of which had been built on the site of the old Plaza Cinema.

The Top Rank Suite's exterior was made from cement blocks. It was square, hulking, geometric, grey. Across the road was a multi-storey car park, equally grey and utilitarian. The Top Rank's entrance was guarded by a pair of bouncers who would look you over carefully and ask your age.

The Top Rank was enormous, like nothing else in Swansea, before or since. On the lowest level there were approximately three bars and here no questions were asked about the buyer's age. In the centre was the main dance floor, which was the size of a large school playground and was overlooked on the furthest wall by a stage where the DJ was enthroned.

To the right were the ladies' powder room, the cloakroom and the gents. *Powder Room* wasn't just a fancy name for the toilets, as the place did boast a large room fitted out with banks of illuminated mirrors and long dressing tables with specially designed insets that were meant to hold boxes of tissues, although all of them were empty. The light in there was glaring, and it was here that fights between girls often flared up, suggesting that these had to be hidden, or at least only seen by other women.

From the powder room there was a door that led into the ladies' toilet with its rows of cubicles, sinks and more mirrors. You could leave the toilets by a separate door which led back towards the dance floor; the design made it a good place for a situation comedy or a useful way of evading pursuers, be they unwanted boys or aggressive girls. The latter category was of course less easily shaken off and again this may be why fights tended to break out in the powder room.

On the left, running parallel with the dance floor was one of the largest drinks bars and beyond that an area with another smaller dance floor, another bar and a food area where you could buy hamburgers, hot dogs, chips and *Chicken in the Basket*. Near the food counter was another set of toilets, gents and ladies, and a flight of stairs leading up to the next level. These stairs were both shorter and deeper than ordinary stairs, forcing the walker to adjust their normal step to accommodate them. They too were carpeted. The carpet must have soaked up the sops and spillage of a thousand beers and ciders, but in the dim light it looked perfectly presentable, even if it was a little sticky underfoot.

These stairs and others around the place led to what was called the balcony. It was far more than a balcony really, rather it was a whole second floor, with bars and toilets in many of the same places as directly below, but here, instead of the large dance floor, there was a great square hole so that you could watch the stage or get a bird's eye view of the dancers directly below. On this floor there was also another smallish dance floor with illuminated tiles underfoot.

On Friday and Saturday nights the place was packed. Outside, on the other side of the road there were usually six or more coaches parked which had brought revellers in groups from Neath and Ammanford and the Valleys.

There was a strict dress code – almost unthinkable for such a place now: no denim, no leather; smart dress only. And so the place was jam-packed with smartly dressed young people giving the rather false impression that their behaviour too would be flawless; but the white shirts got bespattered with blood, the dresses torn, the tights snagged and laddered, the hair ripped out, the smart suit-jackets vomited on.

Debra and I had similar shoes to one another at the time: platform-soles with high heels, sling-backs and a pattern of three broad stripes across the part that covered the toes and lower foot. Mine were red, yellow and navy; hers were brown, tan and beige.

Back then all of the girls wore coats when they arrived, and checked them into the cloakroom. All of the girls had handbags, which couldn't be parted with as they contained money, make-up, hairbrush, hairspray, cloakroom ticket and house keys. If, like Debra and me, there were only two of you, then while dancing you had no choice but to put your handbags together on the floor and dance around them, being careful to ensure no one kicked them to one side in order to steal them.

We'd dance together for record after record, hoping some boys would come and dance with us. The boys came, but not often, two of them tapping us on the shoulder mid-song. We would turn and face our respective boys, directing our bodies at them and then continue the dancing.

I never found love there despite all my efforts. Not love and not a boyfriend either. There were dances with boys, and there were kisses and slow smooches, and sometimes veritable wrestling matches with over-eager boys whose hands ducked and dived and delved and dallied only to be pushed, slapped, elbowed and wriggled away from.

The Rank closed at one in the morning, but Debra's curfew was for twelve so we had to leave before the night was over and, having no money, we walked with aching, burning feet across the Kingsway, up Christina Street, then turned left onto Walters Road and followed it all the way to the Uplands where Debra lived.

At that age it seemed we spent hours walking from one place to another. Side by side we'd go, never linking arms as some girls did, fearing the accusation of *lesbo!* which we'd heard often enough from boys when we'd refused to dance or drink with them.

Often we walked in fear. The attention we so desperately sought from boys often came unwanted from men. These men might be simply kind, offering us a lift. Some might fall into step beside us, offering to walk with us. Some would lean from cars and lorries, yelling anything from *Hey gorgeous!* to *Nice tits*. Or there might be wolf whistles. The worst encounters were with the strange men who lurked in bushes or behind railings with their trousers open, exposing themselves. Our tried and tested response to all of these was to stare straight ahead, lift our chins and quicken our pace. *Walk – don't run. Don't talk to strangers. Don't get in someone's car if you don't know them. Don't get in the car even if they say they are a workmate of your dad's. Even if there is a woman in the car –*

we'd learned that much via our parents, from the Moors Murders.

We had a habit of walking with our arms crossed in front, as if somehow by containing our breasts, controlling and concealing them, we might protect ourselves. At that time of night back then, there weren't many cars and very few people on foot. Perhaps later, after the Rank had closed, there would have been a few more people about, just as there would have been earlier after the pubs had closed and people wended their way home. The walk took us about half an hour or less. We wouldn't be drunk, perhaps only tipsy, with just a few half-pints of cider in us, which had mostly been danced away.

Walters Road was a wide thoroughfare with tall terraces on either side, many of which housed the offices of solicitors, estate agents, accountants and chartered surveyors. It rose steadily as we headed for the Uplands just as the name of the area suggested it should. Although above the Uplands, indeed soaring above it, as if to disprove the geographical tag, was the sprawling housing estate of Townhill.

On the right we passed St James, a church buried deep amongst generous grounds and hidden behind many tall trees. We walked on the left side of the road, hurrying now, but not because of the curfew – rather with an impatience to release our feet from the crippling bondage of our platform shoes. Sometimes our night ended with the two of us sitting in Debra's parlour with our tights and shoes off, and our raw sticky feet soaking in a plastic bowl of cooling water.

Just after the church on the left was a modest-sized purpose-built block of flats called Belgrave Court and it was here a few years earlier that we had seen one of our several flashers lurking in the sparse shrubbery alongside the building. It had happened in broad daylight and the man was barely concealed from the busy road. I had only taken a glimpse and saw that his face was concealed by something that Debra later insisted was a mask and I thought had been a red handkerchief or scarf. And then there was his penis: a flaccid, pink, alien thing offered in the palm of his hand as if it were a gift or something to be inspected; the butcher showing his best pork sausages for the housewife's approval, the child with a flower.

That day Debra had nudged me, calling attention to the man, 'Don't look,' she hissed, 'walk faster.' We increased our pace, pulses racing, breathing rapidly, barely daring to glance around, to look back to see if he was following. We didn't report it. Never told the police, just forgot about it till the next time. That had happened when we were about fourteen – now we were sixteen, seventeen: older, wiser, bolder, but every bit as vulnerable.

After Belgrave Court there was a road that turned sharply left, taking traffic back in the direction of town. Somewhere between the flats and this turning a car had slowed its pace and was creeping along level with us. It was white and of an unusual make. I glanced over and saw a man, whom I took to be one of my teachers from school, who I knew lived in the vicinity of the Uplands.

Of course, cars slowed down like this when they were lost: they would pull up, and the driver would lean over, roll down the window on the passenger side then ask for some street you'd never heard of.

So I looked at the man again, breaking the rules we had set ourselves to avoid eye contact at all costs; was it the teacher, or did he want directions? I saw, although there was an element of doubt, that it wasn't the person I knew. But I must also have seen something in his expression that told me he wasn't lost. Debra, ever the mistrustful hisser of warnings, had urged me not to look and to hurry away.

We quickened our pace and stared resolutely ahead, but despite this, his car continued to roll along beside us at a slow speed. We walked and he drove for perhaps thirty yards like this until, finally giving up, the man revved his engine and pulled away from us. Except that he didn't go on along the road that led to the Uplands and Gower, but took a sharp turning into the road that led back towards town. This confirmed our opinion on two matters: he wasn't being kind – he clearly wasn't offering us a lift because we were headed in the same direction, and he certainly hadn't been my teacher.

(The teacher in question was a man of around thirty. His hair was reddish-brown and he had a moustache and sideburns, but no beard. The man in the car wasn't him, but someone who clearly resembled him.)

Debra and I hurried on to the Grove where she lived, and we let ourselves into the house. We may have made ourselves tea and toast; we may have soaked our aching feet in bowls of hot water. We may have sat up talking about the events of the night, though it's doubtful, once we had reached safety, that the kerb crawler would have even entered our minds again.

That same night, two other girls had gone together to the Top Rank Suite. Two friends, bosom pals the same age as Debra and me. Two girls from a small village to the east of Swansea, while we were from the west. Two girls who were not quite beautiful, not quite plain; just like Debra and me. Two girls who were probably still holding on to their virginity. Back when virginity was a sort of defence.

Debra and I might have stood elbow to elbow at the bar

with those other two girls, Geraldine and Pauline. We may have danced near each other. Peed in the next toilet cubicle. Sat near each other in the powder room, applying an extra layer of Rimmel mascara or dabbing Avon's cream perfume behind our ears.

Our lives and their lives were empty pages. Our futures uncertain. Our hopes would have been modest, shortsighted. I could not imagine at that age the woman I would become. I thought vaguely that one day there would be marriage, children and a home. In September of 1973 I had just turned seventeen and thought that maybe if I was lucky, I might get into Art College, but after? *After* was a distant dream, a place I would only recognise when I reached it.

Geraldine and Pauline had a slightly later curfew than Debra and I, and much further to walk in order to get home. They left the Top Rank Suite together at one o'clock and turned right where we had turned left, then they had walked across town and after either hitchhiking or being offered a lift, were seen getting into a white van or car. The following morning their bodies were found on waste ground near Llandarcy, an industrial area halfway between Swansea and Neath.

Is this the way the hand of fate works its cruel machinery? Two girls turning left to walk along one road are saved, while two others turn right and are lost? Maybe if Debra and I had lived further away we'd have been more inclined to step gratefully into a stranger's car. We'd have smiled. He would have smiled too. Maybe because he was so much older, a man in his thirties, he would even have scolded us, 'You girls ought to be more careful, walking the streets at this time of night – there's nutters out there you know.'

Maybe he would have promised to drive the girls all the

way home. Strangers can be kind; it is not beyond the realm of possibility. And see how he insists that the girl in the front puts on her safety belt. So caring, so careful. And there are two of them and only one of him. They wouldn't do this if they were alone. That would be silly. That would be dangerous. They would know about that poor girl who was killed back in the summer, Sandra Newton. But she had been alone and thus was far more vulnerable.

The car races through the night, taking them away from Swansea, through the east side, past the docks and the Cape Horner pub, past the Ford production works and on through Jersey Marine.

Soon they will be home. Soon, like Debra and me, they will be able to ease their feet from the pinching punishing shoes. Soon they can sleep.

When does it all go wrong? When do they begin to feel the rising panic, the fear that tonight, of all the nights when they have accepted lifts, they have made a wrong choice? Not perhaps until the very last moment.

He takes a turning up a side road.

'Short cut,' he tells them mildly, 'I know all the short cuts, have to in my work.'

He'll call them 'girls' or 'love' or 'darling', the endearments which signal kindness and affection.

The road here is narrower, rougher, the car will jounce and jostle. 'Oops,' he'll say, 'alright there in the back, love?'

The girl in the front will crane her neck; meet the other's eyes. She'll be signalling danger. One of them might bunch her keys in her fist, just in case. They know about rapists. They are not stupid and there are two of them. But still they take no action. They are on a country lane, barely lit, with no other cars, no nearby houses, no traffic lights that force him to stop so that they can leap from the car and run. But he has explained himself. It's a short cut, that's all.

But then he stops the car, pulls up in a lay-by and their fate is sealed.

No one can know what happened. Or rather, what happened is known; it is the *how* that remains unanswered.

The 'how' is not a desire for salacious detail. The 'how' is about one man overpowering two girls. The 'how' is really a lesson in survival: how to avoid becoming a victim, how to escape.

Was there no chance for either of them once they had stepped into that car? If they had refused the lift would the story be the same? Would every terrible detail remain except for the names of the victims? Instead of Geraldine and Pauline might it have been Julie and Theresa, or Jane and Yvonne?

In 1998 developments in DNA sampling allowed scientists to discover a partial DNA profile of the girls' killer, and this led in 2000 to the reinvestigation of the murders, Operation Magnum. Further tests showed that the same man had been responsible for not only Geraldine and Pauline's murders, but that of Sandra Newton too. The police focused on a shortlist of suspects who had been interviewed in the Seventies, and with the help of a psychological profile of the killer, narrowed it down to one man who had died twelve years earlier, Joseph Kappen. By first obtaining DNA samples from Kappen's children and then exhuming his body, a match was found and the case was solved.

News reports, first in the Swansea *Evening Post* and then in the *Guardian*, revealed the killer's face: he had what looked like reddish brown hair that grew to just below the collar, a

Mexican moustache, and no beard. Looking at that face I had the sensation I had seen it before. My teacher from long ago or someone like him: the man behind the steering wheel of a white car. The man who played the role of a generous stranger who wanted us to accept his kindness, to take the last journey of our lives. Perhaps. Or perhaps not.

Despite the murders of three girls, Debra and I continued to go to the Top Rank and we were there the following Saturday. We passed the bouncers at the door; we descended the first flight of stairs and paid our money. Then went down the next flight to come face to face with several policemen who were sitting at makeshift desks. Were we here last week? 'Yes.' Did we see these girls? 'No.' Did we know them? 'No.' Did we see anything strange last week? Any men acting oddly? 'Well yes, there was this kerb crawler....' We told the story briefly, gave our names and addresses, telephone numbers, and were asked if we would be willing to make full statements.

A young policeman called later in the week. My mother gave him tea and biscuits and installed us in the best room. I told him everything I remembered about that night and he wrote it down in the calculated and alien language of official documents, then read it back to me before I signed my name. When Geraldine and Pauline were last seen, it was beginning to rain. I don't remember it being wet that night but perhaps Debra and I were lucky, and made it home before the rain.

Ravin', I'm Ravin'

Sadie Kiernan

Being a teenager in rural south-west Wales in the late Eighties and early Nineties didn't allow for much rebelling. As a child, I found I was mixing with English migrants who had come to Wales not, it would seem, to live off the land and become at one with their surroundings, but to create a subculture of middle-class *groovy* people who generally had a lot of kids, wore really dreadful ethnic clothes, had old houses that were desperately in need of repair, tidying and most certainly a good clean, with dilapidated caravans/sheds containing further hippies, cannabis plants and patchouli joss sticks. Rebelling by dropping out was not an option: it had been done to death.

Despite being so at one with the earth, their environment and the ancient cultures and traditions surrounding them, these immigrants seemed somehow not to notice that the language of the people who had lived in Wales for centuries was not in fact English. Generally they made no attempt to encourage their children to learn Welsh or mix with Welsh-speaking families, and the notion that they themselves might perhaps learn even a little, or even attempt to pronounce place names properly, apparently did not occur to them.

Part of my early rebellion took the form of studying the playground Welsh I'd learned to GCSE and A-Level as a first language, and taking my other subjects through the medium of Welsh as a mother tongue. Partly to show the immigrants how rude and ignorant they were, and partly to show the Welsh natives that not only did I have the courtesy and intelligence to learn their language, but that I was in fact better at it than many of the minority who still speak it. Such was my arrogance.

I remained top of the class until I started smoking dope at around fourteen; typically at home, with my folks, in front of *Coronation Street*. There was clearly no point in the parents laying down the law about drug taking and unconventional behaviour, when it was their way of life.

At this point I discovered another, more exciting way of rebelling against my hippie-lentil-CND upbringing. I started hanging out with nearby council-estate kids who were not into folk music and jamming, but rather hip hop and clubbing. It was at this point that I began to notice the relative merits of having had a broad and open-minded introduction to drugs, partying and festival-going, even though in my circle being a hippie was still rather uncool.

It was with my new posse that I went to my first rave: World Party – Circus & Menagerie in the north of England. I'd been looking forward to it for ages. I was well accustomed to mind-altering drugs, including the much-abused magic mushrooms which could be picked on the nearby Preseli Mountains each September. But taking a pill and going raving was something altogether else.

The ember of the illegal rave in the UK had been fanned by the emergence of tracks like *We Call it Aceed* in the commercial music scene when I was in my early teens. Fuelled by amphetamine-based drugs, in particular MDMA/MDA (ecstasy), there was an inferno of illegal and subsequently legal raves up and down the country. The essential factor, though, as with any significant sub-culture, was the youths, who hailed from a region of outstanding natural beauty but high unemployment and little opportunity. This post-sexual-revolution generation of kids were intent on some kind of momentous uprising but were also seeking to avoid personal feelings of insignificance and alienation through the euphoric sense of togetherness that such drugs create. In simple terms, the nutty ravers had fuck-all to lose, so threw themselves into roaming around the UK in pursuit of drugs and a bpm of anything over a hundred and thirty.

Ecstasy for me was the ultimate form of escape. It brought a sense of elation, inclusion, clarity, peace, oneness, exhilaration, touchy-feeliness; a need to love, touch and be loved and touched, and compassion, cut with a rushing fuelled by amphetamine and enhanced by sexual desire and a sense of invincibility. All this was topped with intense hallucinations brought about by a skaggy, LSD-laced E, or a level of intoxication so high that you simply existed in another dimension for a few hours, where time, distance and what your eyes saw inside your head was removed from reality. The bodily sensations that accompanied this inspired a consciousness and sense of synchronicity with, er, the Universe....

There was of course a huge amount of coming down to

be had, including nausea, headaches, paranoia, anxiety, depression, sweats, total lack of money, rapid deterioration of key relationships – the usual. But fuck that, right, if you can just get fucked off your face every weekend travelling around the country with a load of like-minded youths who also like to dance and fuck a lot. That was the bottom line rationale at the time....

As things progressed we soon became aware that living in south-west Wales was not in fact a disadvantage, even though we might be largely cut off from the source of all coolness: London. This was where all the big name DJs came from, where all the well-known clubs, record/clothes shops were, where all the best drugs could be found, and, without a doubt, where all the most exciting and ground-breaking new music was originating – break beat hardcore, jungle, drum n bass, House and UK dance music like Soul II Soul, Rebel MC, SL2, Ragga Twins, the Prodigy, Inner City, and Cold Cut, and DJs such as Carl Cox, Grooverider, Fabio and Jumping Jack Frost.

We soon found throngs of inner-city dwellers venturing far outside their comfort zone into the depths of rural Wales, where large-scale parties were being assembled in fields, barns, sand dunes, and on hills, almost every weekend.

We had one party on Freshwater West beach, not far from Pembroke, where the national surfing championships were sometimes held. It has a long sandy beach and miles of sand dunes, and an army shooting range behind the beach cut it off from any towns or interfering authorities/straight people. It was surprisingly well attended, considering it clashed with a big legal rave in Oxford. Our reputation far and wide had seemingly pulled in the usual range of full crew from the aforementioned areas, together with many scuzzy traveller types and trust-afarians (trust-fund drop-outs).

The rave was held in the centre of a rather huge sand dune which was shaped like a high-sided bowl. We used 4x4s and off-road vehicles to manoeuvre the large speakers, a PA system, some decks and a mike, several DJs and crates of beer. There was no food, just drugs – including some Dennis the Menace capsules laced with LSD.

As the sun began to rise over the sea I found myself climbing to the top of the lip of the sand dune bowl with a friend, rushing madly with the exertion as we peered out over the top, then sniffing a nostril full of poppers and reeling with powerful heady hallucinations of a computerised cliff jetty protruding into the vast ocean which was overhung by a gleaming pearlescent moon and shooting stars. I did step out onto the non-existent jetty, plunging like an idiot down the other side of the dune onto the beach, afterwards understanding how people inadvertently kill themselves on drugs. Afterwards my friend and I lay side by side on our backs doing a 'cross-town traffic survey' of all the cars, mainly police cars and gangster mobiles, that were zooming around in the sky just above our heads.

Our mate turned up with his dad's ice cream van, to the delight of the drug-crazed ravers whose stomachs had become those of junkies, finding ice cream the best type of food to digest. It was also great fun to offer some googly-eyed buzzed-up freak on the dance floor a lick of your 99 then shove it in their reddened sweaty huffing and puffing face.

One of the major attractions of this event was the bouncy castle. Fairground rides were a loved-up raver's idea of heaven, particularly kiddy ones: those with no sharp edges. I once sat in a cup and saucer mini-roundabout ride with my pal Dave, me in the cup, him in the saucer, going very very slowly holding hands and gawping like idiots at the entire set of the Prodigy as we came up on two rather strong White Doves. It was deep.

I also remember hallucinating in an unusually creative way that evening, where all the men I was dancing with – men I knew, and the ones with beards – had on women's clothing and full makeup.

At the end of the night my best friend Ruth and I sat in my car. I was in the passenger seat with my head reclined and my eyes rolling wildly, open to a slit – I knew the car was stationery, and yet I kept drifting into this kind of motion illusion where we were speeding down a busy motorway. I'd wake up with a jolt to Ruth's surprise as she gurned and stared confoundedly at the wheel, having entirely forgotten how to make it turn. Apparently we remained there for over an hour.

Having hired a bouncy castle, one of the major features of the night was when someone lit up a joint near one of the pipes and the whole thing just ignited. It was very pretty and ridiculously funny, but one person did end up having to go to hospital with an asthmatic fit from the weird fumes it gave off. I guess that was one of the reasons why these parties were illegal.

The illegality of the raves was part of the attraction – it was an underground scene. But it also ended up being a problem, since there were invariably a few people set on scamming the rest. And, unfortunately, the goodwill that was extended by my family, who allowed me to hold a massive rave on our estate in the Shed (the barn where they have always held gigs, jams and parties), ended up getting abused when I held my last big rave at home on my twenty-first birthday.

I started off with a thousand Doves to sell and the hope that the party would be well enough attended for me to enjoy the celebration. Within an hour I found myself standing at the door saying, 'Excuse me, this is my party and I don't know who you are.' I gave up soon after. The whole length of our quarter-mile track, every parking space and verge, was bumper to bumper with cars from as far afield as Cardiff. Unfortunately the next day, when we were all passed out down at the house and some ravers came back to acquire the decks and sound equipment, they found it gone. So they took all the backdrops and lighting as a consolation prize.

I now live in London where I DJ, am involved in the music industry and still very much enjoy raving as often as possible, although I now omit the drugs and focus largely on the dancing. This is because my body forced me to wake up quick-time and address rather directly the nature of my self-destructive ways.

I now watch young people of all ages taking all sorts of so-called Es, coke, MDMA. The contents of this stuff are very far from what it says on the packet. Additionally, since their price has dropped rapidly, and given the rate of inflation since I used to buy them, it's logical to assume that the quality of the drugs has dropped significantly.

I also know inside myself that should I even once decide to risk taking these chemicals as a treat or to reminisce, the inevitable anxiety about how ill it might make me would cancel any feelings of euphoria.

I stay in touch with quite a few of my friends from my raving years in Wales, partly because they come from my home patch, and partly because I like to believe the post-hippie generation – like their forebears – have a bond through drugs, music and culture.

Occasionally I wonder if the volume of drugs I took during my hedonistic hallucinogenic escapologist trip as a pioneer of Welsh raving may have damaged me profoundly. But I don't regret these phenomenal experiences and how some dimension of my perception remains perpetually influenced by them.

Anyone who chooses to get involved in drug abuse is using it as a form of release, an escape. It was an expression: a form of communication that didn't rely on language or background – it connected us all to a sense of freedom, and this in a uniquely stunning natural setting. It also disconnected us, for a while, from the horrible notion that we would have to one day take responsibility for our lives.

Dumping Stucky

Rachel Trezise

I wanted real adventures to happen to myself. But real adventures, I reflected, do not happen to people who remain at home: they must be sought abroad.

James Joyce, *Dubliners*

In 1999, I turned twenty. I still lived in the Rhondda and the Rhondda was the same place it had always been: villages full of grey-skinned benefit recipients who talked about it like it was the centre of the universe and its population the salt of the Earth. What I saw was obese women who thought nothing of shopping in their pyjamas and teenagers on hard drugs. It was a vicious hand-to-mouth cycle and if there were roads out of it people didn't have the opportunity to take them. It was a decade since my step-father had raped me and six years since he was found not guilty. My vain, gold-digging mother had lost her looks to alcohol abuse and was therefore drinking more heavily than ever. Reminders of my abysmal 'upbringing' were all around. The village was a pot-hole in a mountain, the life trapped inside it, stagnant.

I was going to leave. My first plan of escape had been hampered when I failed my English A-Level. I was set to elope to Cornwall, where I'd study literature by day and gut fish by night, all the while quickly becoming someone who wasn't Welsh, for this feature embarrassed me vastly. I could reinvent myself by enrolling at a far-flung establishment of education. Simply going elsewhere could make me normal and glamorous, I was sure. But because of my failed exam, only the local university would have me. All things considered, it wasn't a bad university, it was respected and its reputation was growing. But I was still in Wales. I caught the train home every night to my terraced parental home, rarely participating in any social events at the union. Then, one day at the beginning of my sophomore year, a tutor asked me if I wanted to study abroad for six months, and I saw my route to freedom laid out before me like a celestial yellow brick road.

The first thing I saw when I arrived in Dublin was a record shop with a black and white print of BB King tacked to the window. The shop's woodwork was painted green and its interior blacked out with dark muslin. It's how I imagined Chicago, because I'd never been to Chicago, I'd never been anywhere. I would have liked to have stayed in Dublin because it was full of literature and history. When I'd pushed myself out of my class barrier I could go to dinner parties and say, 'Oh yes darling, I studied at Trinity.' I wasn't staying though – I had another six-hour train journey to endure, at the end of which I'd arrive in the red light area of a place nick-named Stab City. Limerick.

I shared a hostel with two hundred other students, most of them Irish, but lots from the USA, some from Europe and one from Wales. I'd met Morgan once at Pontypridd University, a plump girl from the Vale of Glamorgan, a Sweater Shop logo stretching across her enormous tits. In our new country she'd found me on the hostel forecourt, staring at a chalky Virgin Mary statuette I'd spotted hiding behind the shrubbery. We explored our new university together. It was called Mary Immaculate College; a small townhouse with tin annexes sprawling out of its orifices. The building was celebrating its centenary – originally it was a staunch Catholic institution where girls studied teaching. There was a nunnery and the Sisters of Mercy shared the third floor. It had its own church with two receptacles of holy water on either side of the door. Irish students dipped their fingers in and crossed themselves each time they passed it, and they passed it ten or more times a day.

At our first lecture, it was Morgan who noticed the locked television cabinet at the front of the hall, and the note pinned to it, which said, The key to this cupboard is on the top shelf in room 53.

'I'm not being funny,' she said, 'but that's why the Irish get called backward.'

On St David's Day morning I was woken by the mean and aggravating sound of somebody else's hardcore sex. The bedposts in the room next door knocked against the wall, a few inches away from my head. I reached for one of the felt daffodils Morgan had her mother send us in the post and fingered it, popping the safety pin in the stem open and closed, trying not to visualise what was going on in the next bedroom but doing it all the same. I tried to imagine little children on their way to school concerts, the boys dressed as miners, dirt smudged on their ruddy cheeks, the girls in chequered shawls.

A month before I'd left, I'd met a new boyfriend in the local pub. There was a darts match on, and they had a buffet. He had winked at me over the left-over faggot sandwiches. At closing time he drove me, drunk, to the flat above his father's shop. His father was the local tattooist. He wasn't a good tattooist. He'd made a living out of misspelled names driven into the wrists of minors. All his black ink turned after a year into a mossy colour. I scanned some of the more attractive designs for five minutes, the Celtic bracelets and Chinese lettering, then went upstairs and took my clothes off. I directed his fingertip to my clitoris and he stabbed it awkwardly while I spread out over the damp single bed. Soon enough, he lost it again. It turned out we didn't have sex, not then. He was celebrating a year clean of heroin, he said, and I wasn't sure if that had anything to do with his flaccid, circumcised penis, or if he was just making conversation. Images visited me in REM sleep of myself in threadbare underwear, sliding around a steel dancer's pole, wide eyes and salivating mouths following every puny movement, and there in the background, this man, Stucky, smiling on the scenario with feverish, shining pride.

The way he'd swooned at the sight of my naked body and called me stunning (I was quite ordinary), stared, open-mouthed, his tongue poking out in concentration as I spoke: it made him appear feeble. His desperation would make a relationship impossible. There'd be no challenge in it, no higher place to aspire to – he already adored me. I'd get everything I wanted and I'd be bored in less than a year. I didn't even fancy him for long. He was fat, with an upturned nose and a slight hunchback. He was twenty-five but looked and acted fifty. Yet something in my psyche was attracted to him. The idea of having somebody who cared about me waiting at home for my return was a comforting one. It wouldn't be my mother – she'd warned me amid an alcohol-fuelled rage that if I abandoned her now (she'd suddenly become bed-ridden and needed me to go out every day for cheap whiskey), Ireland wasn't far enough away. Leaving the only place I'd ever known became a scary prospect – I'd be like a kite with no handle and no string. So I traded the little bit of sympathy I did feel for him in exchange for security. Just in case I did come back.

After a week in Limerick, I rang him. He was emotional from the outset, sniffling before he spoke.

'What's the matter with you?' I said.

'Oh, it's stupid,' he said. I imagined the phone line under the sea, stretching through the earth to where his sausage fingers were wiping his cheeks. 'I got stuck behind the free Tesco bus today, and I haven't stopped crying since. Do you know what the free Tesco bus is called?'

'The Shamrock Shopper?' I said.

'Yeah –'

I heard torrents of tears flood his voice. And he was right, it was stupid.

'I have to go now,' I said. 'I'll ring you next week.'

Aaron, one of the Americans, a skinny boy with an Adam's apple poking out of his swanlike neck, had appeared in the corridor and was smiling at me. He tapped his shower sandal on the terracotta floor, play-acting impatient, the woody scent of his after-shave defeating the tea-time smell of pasta sauce from the kitchen. His skin was a healthy olive colour, his eyes a soft brown. His attention made me want to end the clingy, tasteless conversation I was having with Stucky and begin my new life in Ireland. I felt a tingly sensation reach up into my face. I was meeting new people now. I didn't need Stucky anymore. His sanctuary was already defunct and the adventure I'd been looking for was about to begin.

'I love you,' Stucky said.

I put the phone down.

Stucky chose to subsidise my government grant so I could afford a social life: he sent me chocolates in the post and he worked in a library and stole all my text-books for me. In the same way he had helped buy my ticket out of Wales, I hoped Aaron would be my ticket out of Ireland – another step across another ocean, because all Americans lived in beachside mansions with en-suites. He could take me home to meet his mother.

I soon discovered, however, that Aaron wasn't rich. He worked illegally, washing gravy off the dishes in Dolan's, the nearby pub-restaurant, to pay for his food and clothing. He lived in Chesapeake Bay but studied business at Frostburg University in Maryland: 'Marilyn', as he called it, adding an inflection to his sugary American lilt. His English grandparents had emigrated to the US in the late 1940s and he'd come to Ireland in the hope of saving enough to make a trip over to London to watch Arsenal play.

'I've only got two pairs of training shoes,' he said, 'and most Americans have seven.' Nevertheless, I quickly became besotted with him because he was everything that Stucky and every other boy I'd known in Wales wasn't. He was ambitious. He wanted to open a bistro in Washington. Gourmet on a budget, he called it. On a Thursday, when he got paid, he cooked peppers stuffed with broccoli and sweet potatoes, or pancakes with apple puree, and brought them into the common room with a charred tea-towel over his forearm. Most men in the Valleys spent their twenties chasing the dragon in a bid to forget that they were alive. Aaron was the first boyfriend I had who was making an effort to prolong, even improve his life.

In the first half of the semester he'd take me to the fleapit cinema in the city and we'd watch movies, eating caramel chocolates, his lanky legs bunched up onto the burgundy velveteen seat. The theatre was always empty on weeknights; customers had long moved on to the new Multiplex in Ennis. It was a rare opportunity for us to be alone but we never said very much to one another. I didn't want to tell him about my embarrassing past so we spent a lot of time smiling through the glare of the screen. One time on the way home we kissed, Aaron getting so zealous he dropped the umbrella he was holding above us and we stayed for ten minutes, our tongues sprawling around in our toffee-flavoured saliva, the Irish rain aiming at us like needles. On the third date he came to my room afterwards. I didn't know if it was my anticipation or Aaron's skill but I had my first orgasm. At least I thought that's what it was. It was stronger than any sexual climaxes I'd experienced earlier but moderate compared to the results of masturbation – something I learned much later.

Afterwards, our acquaintance became distant. I saw him in history lectures where he wrote notes to me on scraps of foolscap paper, postponing our next arrangement. Time was running out, he said, the semester ended in June and he still hadn't been to London; he needed to keep saving. He always seemed to be working. When I did catch glimpses of him at home, he was always surrounded by other girls. The first years from the third floor sat around him at the breakfast table while they stuffed toast-halves into their mouths, staring doe-eyed at him, which made me want to whip a meat knife out of its block and plant it firmly between their shoulder-blades. I noticed one day that one of them, Roisín, a short girl who wore a tiny tie-dyed sarong to and from the bathroom, was wearing his shower sandals. At 4am the following morning I knocked on his bedroom door. Chris, his dormitory-mate answered, his hands crossed defensively across his naked chest. 'No,' he said, 'I thought he was with you.' Exasperated by his absence I went out on Friday night in my one and only little black dress. It had a slit on the left side which exposed the lace top of my 10 denier hold-ups. I purposely walked through the common-room on my way out. The fourth year Irish students who had been watching Eddie Irvine win a motor race looked away from the television and securely planted their gaze on my legs. But Aaron wasn't even there. Aaron was never there. Three cocktails in, sitting alone and self-conscious in a hotel bar on O'Connor Street, I resolved to win him back with sheer persistence. I was still dreaming about America and I'd get there by wearing that dress until the very day he came back to my room and ripped it off.

This plan was especially difficult to execute because of Stucky's insistence on purchasing a super-saver travel voucher from the Pembroke to Rosslare Ferry. He visited me four times in six months. On the first three occasions I hid him in my bedroom and writhed out of his advances by allowing the flea-ridden hostel cat to sleep on my pillow between us. On his fourth visit he drove me to a plush hotel in Galway where I spent the weekend miserable and secretly pining for Aaron. The only way to quell the frustration was to finally let Stucky fuck me and even this was a failure. He thrust into the hollow where my abdomen ended and my right leg began, missing both orifices altogether, his movement aided by my sweat, his eyes wide and unsure, as though he'd heard he won the lottery but knew it had to be a joke.

When I got back to the hostel we were three quarters of the way through the semester. Coming out of the kitchen with a cucumber sandwich, I saw Aaron sitting in the common room. Unfortunately, I wasn't wearing the dress.

'Hey honey,' he said, turning his sleep-creased face towards me. 'Long time no see.' He smiled playfully and then quickly forgot the gesture. 'You just missed this holiday show all about Wales,' he said excitedly, nodding at the TV.

'Where in Wales?' I said. It was unlikely, even in Limerick, that anyone would choose to spend any of their precious time in the Rhondda, and I hoped that Aaron still had no idea about the shameful industry-pocked wasteland I originated from, because I'd lied and told him it looked like the Gower.

'The Lake District,' he said.

'The Lake District is in the north of England, you dick,' I said. 'Are you thick or something?'

'I'm not thick,' he said quickly. 'Know what my favourite TV channel is? Huh? The Discovery Channel! I'm intelligent.'

My colourful fantasies about completing my degree in Maryland, eating key-lime pie on the sunny college lawn between seminars were just that: fancies that made Aaron seem more extraordinary than he was. He might have been ambitious, but he was still as dense as pig-shit; an all-American boy looking for a good time, and that, although admirable compared to Stucky, fell short of my requirements. I put my saucer down on the table and rubbed my palms free of crumbs.

In April we went to see a rugby match, Morgan and me, England versus Wales. I didn't like rugby, I was more into football. Neither did Morgan. Still, it seemed like the appropriate thing to do. If we were in Wales, that's what we'd do: pretend to like it, watch it, because that's what everyone else was doing.

Rain water dripped from my coat to the floor. The sawdust absorbed it.

'Are you showing the Wales/England match?' Morgan asked, catching her breath. The barman was resting his swollen stomach on the bar between two Guinness pumps. I climbed up onto the barstool. The room was cold, the storm outside pelting the roof.

'Why would ya be wantin' ta watch a Wales an' Ingland match, now?' he said, his patent black eyes shining through his rippled skin.

'Because I'm Welsh,' I said.

'Are ya?' he said.

'Yeah.'

'Where're ya from?' he said quickly, as though he didn't believe I was Welsh and was trying to catch me out.

'The Rhondda,' I replied, quickly. He couldn't get me on where I came from. The Rhondda was as Welsh as it got. We had more emphysema claims from ex-coal miners per household than rats. And a male voice choir. I was wearing my *Manic Street Preachers* T-shirt, a red skinny rib with **VALLEY GIRL** emblazoned across my flat bust in bold, white characters. I shrugged my coat off my shoulders to reveal it.

Having seemed to lose the argument the man abruptly turned the volume up on the remote control.

'Now look out for Dean,' Morgan said, lifting her pint of stout and sipping the ecru-coloured froth. 'He's in Wembley on a stag weekend.' The game was already halfway through and England were winning. I lazily scanned the stands for Morgan's boyfriend and a face I recognised stood out unexpectedly from the crowd. It wasn't Dean, it was Ieuan: a monstrously tall ex-junkie with dreadlocks falling around his waist, who lived at the top of my village. He was known to have injected the old brown with Stucky on many an occasion. He was wearing a *Manic Street Preachers* T-shirt with **VALLEY BOY** emblazoned across his pigeon chest.

'That's Ieuan,' I said turning, enlivened, to Morgan. 'He's from my village.' She didn't answer so I looked at her face. 'I know him, honestly.' It was like trying to convince her that Marilyn Monroe was my grandmother. Suddenly it meant a great deal that Morgan believed I knew that man. That man, who in Wales I'd cross the road to avoid.

It was important now that she knew I'd found a clear sense of identity. Whenever she'd asked me about the Rhondda I'd told her as little as possible. I didn't want her to know about the used needles in the playgrounds or the cut-price wine bottles littering the streets. I didn't want her to know about the unemployment and economic breakdown which had caused the crime and domestic abuse statistics to rocket. I'd wanted her to think that I came from somewhere normal. At the beginning I'd thought Limerick would be normal and that it could make me normal, that it could wash my experiences of child abuse out of my mind, but Limerick wasn't normal. It was violent and dull. Travel had taught me that there was no such thing as normal. There was no miraculous eraser that could scrub my birthplace off my birth certificate and no medical procedure to make my memories extinct. So I was learning to accept the Rhondda, and with it myself. The next time I saw Ieuan on the street I wouldn't deliberately shun him. I was proud of him; proud that he'd ventured out of his mouldy flat with a **VALLEY BOY** T-shirt on instead of injecting smack; proud that today at least, he wanted to live.

'I do,' I said. 'I know him.'

'Okay,' she said aggressively.

For the next half hour it was a close-set match. I balanced on the harsh rim of my stool, the soles of my pumps sliding down its aluminium legs, my skin burning anxiously. Wales scored a try to bring us equal but Jenkins missed the conversion. Then England scored a try and we were almost into injury time. Although it was actually the first time I'd done it, I felt as though I'd spent my whole life watching red jerseys scrum up to white.

Much of the graffiti in Ireland claimed that God Brought the Great Famine and England Did The Rest, a grudge passed through generations like chromosomes. Shop assistants refused penny coins because the Queen's head was shaped into the copper, and never mind that they were the same size, or that they were worth more than their money. I was becoming proud and patriotic and all the things I should have been while I still had the rest of Wales around me to agree. Maybe I was old enough and bitter enough, like the men who sang IRA songs in the Denmark Street Taverns, to want to smash England's complacent face in. England and Empire had caused the emergence of coal mines in the Rhondda, and their eventual demise: two injustices which had left me critical and confused about my place of origin. What I was sure of though, was that I was Welsh. And I'd come to understand it, like the Irish had, by not being English: my identity was determined in relation to what I was not.

Out of nowhere, a red shirt got to the try line with the ball in the crook of its arm and magically performed a feat of pure ballet.

'Scott Gibbs,' the commentator said. 'Scott Gibbs is through. Scott Gibbs has scored. What an amazing try!' It was 30-31 with a minute to go. Morgan stood up and then sat down and then stood up.

'Say something, Rachel,' she said.

I shielded my eyes from the screen. 'We might actually win this,' I said.

'You've done it,' the barman said. I opened my eyes just as the ball sailed over the bar. 'You've done it, girls.' Somehow his Irish voice wasn't disturbed enough. We'd beaten England by a hair's-breadth for the first time in eleven years. Morgan wiped her face.

'Well, let's get pissed,' I said.

'Where?' she said. 'Where shall we go?'

Immediately I realised that there was no raucous crowd of rugby supporters to celebrate with. The bar owner had turned the television off and we weren't in England, or Wales. We were in Ireland.

When Morgan got back to Wales two months later, she became a rugby player. When I got home I dumped Stucky.

3

Borderline

Teithio yn y Nos Nachtreise

Patricia Duncker

The last village gleams black and white in the streetlights. I can see the roof of the bell tower just behind the Red Lion. The New Inn rises up in the centre of the road. I slow down, then accelerate past the end of the speed restriction zone, and sweep away down the hill, turn right at the roundabout below Kington, Offa's Dyke is now somewhere above me, then there is nothing between me and the border. The world is never quite dark in the middle of the night. I can see the crouching hills, bare outlines, no trees. There are no other cars and no lights. Once the streetlights vanish into hedges there is only a huge northern night and clouds masking the stars. I watch the sides of the road for hesitating animals. I am now driving fast and silent, confident on the curves, looking for the border. Concentrate. Here it comes. A gulf between two great folds in the hills. It is midnight, and I have crossed from England into Wales.

Now that I work in England and spend far more time travelling back than I ever used to do, I have become sharply aware of the border, its significance and its presence. Wales has become another country, ever more clearly, and its language seems stranger, less familiar. I have the good fortune to live in a part of Wales where Welsh is both spoken casually, as a matter of course, and treasured and defended with an energetic militancy that warms the hearts of European language activists, the advocates of Breton and the *langue d'Oc*. I work as an editor for Honno, a bilingual Welsh press which publishes the work of Welsh women and women who live in Wales. Language and landscape are always interwoven. I whirl silently across the unpeopled frontier from England into Wales and I look out for the language, the double Ls and the distinctive endings. And it is the same in Europe. The first thing I notice as I cross the border from France into Germany is the sign with its coil of stars: Bundesrepublik Deutschland. And here is the natural frontier – the Rhine – peppered with barges and hydro-electric power stations: above me looms the long rise of hills that form the Schwarzwald. I search for the changing place names and street signs. And I am in another country.

My first French visitors to Wales, neither of whom speak any English at all, were wonderfully baffled and enchanted by the Welsh language. They could not recognise the vowels and actually photographed the sign saying, CANOLFAN Y CELFYDDYDAU, because as far as they were concerned it was a language entirely mastered by consonants. Explanations were pointless. They loved the strangeness and the difference.

Borders always signal difference and transition. You are now leaving the English Zone. They also represent division, possession or exclusion. They are never neutral symbols. This is our country, and if you do not have the good fortune to be coming home to the land where you were born, the earth which owns you as one of its children, and the people who remember you when you were small, you are there as a stranger, a foreigner, a visitor, an incomer, a tourist. Your welcome is always uncertain, provisional. I was made to feel that I did not belong when I first moved to Wales in October 1991, and, for the first time, after decades of stealthy or flamboyant border crossings, I became part of a small inward-looking community and knew what it felt like to be a visible stranger. A border may barely be visible, but it may still be deeply acknowledged by those who live on either side. The fact that a border cannot be seen does not mean that it does not exist.

Berlin. Early April, 1970. The Wall has been up for nearly ten years. It is beginning to show signs of its shoddy, sudden construction. Concrete slapped between breeze blocks oozes and cracks. Grass blows on the slits between slabs and rabbits bounce cheerily across the floodlit glare of Potsdamer Platz. Die Mauer, elsewhere in divided Germany known as Die Grenze, encloses a protected zone, sprouting wild life, rare lichens, a quiet, unpolluted space, littered with hidden land mines. We are in love with the possibility of crossing the Wall. We are foreigners in Berlin and we can therefore do it easily. A day pass, two stamps, change a bit of money and over you go, into the huge empty spaces, wide streets with no traffic, black, battered buildings with bullet holes all down the walls, the abandoned desolation of East Berlin. We have been brought up on the novels of Len Deighton and John Le Carré.

We are frontier people; we enter the forbidden cities of fairy tale, confronting ogres with impunity. Not for us the banal security of climbing off the train at Friedrichstrasse, hustled into line with all the other tourists, or anxious West Berliners, visiting Communism. No, we love the thrill of armed soldiers, waiting on the dark platforms of forgotten, locked underground stations, their khaki coats shapeless and mysterious in the gloom. We want our route to be charted with binoculars, our steps menaced by live rounds of ammunition. We want to play at being spies. We are arrogant enough to court the risk of being shot. Soldiers behind us, soldiers before us, we strut jauntily across die Grenze at Checkpoint Charlie, cigarettes alight, talking loudly, super cool.

East Berlin is a massive disappointment. We cannot find a restaurant. The shops do not exist. The people we see on the streets are always scurrying away into the distance. The cathedral is shut, apparently forever. The building has been declared unsafe. It has never recovered from the war. The woman at the ticket office in the Pergamon Museum clearly hates us. I am ticked off by an officious guard for stroking the massive gates of Ishtar, the beautiful golden lions of Babylon, set in luminous oceans of Arabic blue tiles. Naked Greek statues with unbelievably tiny penises litter the gloomy cream vaults. Everything is covered in dust. The smeared glass cases are unlit. Faded, typed labels, browning, peeling off, give us minimal information. What is this? A pot? A plate? Part of a necklace? No one knows. There is no café and the postcards are all black and white.

After this bad experience no one else wants to go to the National Gallery. I go on my own and find that it is shut. Two huge railway sleepers are fixed across the doors. Broken glass

litters the steps. *Unter den Linden* is empty. I watch two
tiny cars puttering off into cobbled back streets taking the
cobblestones in a harrowing sequence of leaps and bumps. I
meet up with my friends again. We are now deflated,
exhausted and frozen. We want to go back to our warm flat in
West Berlin, but we have tickets for the theatre, Goethe's
Faust, Part 1. We must stay on and see the show. We dare not
admit defeat or acknowledge, even to each other, that Berlin
is empty, frightening and very, very, cold, and that we have
not enjoyed ourselves. The sky turns grey, then dark above us
and we retreat, shivering, to the theatre foyer. We must look
like naïve foreigners because everyone gives us a very wide
berth. The East Germans dress up for the theatre so we are
painfully visible. They are all wearing dark jackets, lamé,
stilettos and taffeta. They smell slightly of mothballs. I am
wearing an Afghan waistcoat with tiny mirrors stitched into
patterns and a black mini-skirt above my Puss-in-Boots leather
leggings. I smell of damp goat. The cold outside deepens. We
settle into our cheap balcony seats.

That performance of Goethe's *Faust*, at the Volkstheater in
East Berlin in the early spring of 1970 remains one of the
most extraordinary experiences I have ever had. This was
partly due to the scale of the stage. Faust is discovered leaning
on a lectern surrounded by gigantic aged volumes. The vaults
above him were so vast we could not make out where they
ended. He flung one leather bound book away from the desk
and bellowed,

> *Habe nun, ach! Philosophie,*
> *Juristerei und Medizin,*

Und leider auch Theologie
Durchaus studiert, mit heißem Bemühn.
Da steh' ich nun, ich armer Tor,
Und bin so klug als wie zuvor.

(I've studied now Philosophy,
And Jurisprudence, Medicine,
And even alas! Theology
From end to end with labour keen.
And here, poor fool! with all my lore
I stand, no wiser than before.)

We were bewitched. The opening monologue bristled with all the things we felt: rebellion, rage, frustration, and the determination to escape by any means. Faust was speaking for us, for our generation. The production went in for spectacular special effects, leaping flames and monstrous bangs. The Spirit Faust summoned appeared as a giant projection on the backdrop and his hollow roar, *Wer ruft mir?* made us all shudder. We were however all much warmer inside the theatre and thrilled by the excess of spectacle and emotion flung down before us. At last, something unexpected had rewarded our patience. But evil tidings awaited us at the interval.

In those days you could only get a one-day permit to visit East Berlin. You had to cross the border at the point where you had entered and you had to do it before midnight. Our performance did not end until 11.30. We would never make it back to Checkpoint Charlie before the stroke of twelve when the Wall closed forever. A collective decision was taken to miss the last fifteen minutes of the play and creep out of the packed theatre. But when the moment came I couldn't do it. *Faust* is

not a play I have often seen performed, especially not in the
original German. It is episodic, disturbing, moving, satirical
and scary by turns. It is also about wanting more, more of
everything, more knowledge, more youth, more sex, more life.
The finale of this performance made it clear that this was a
case of judgement and forgiveness, damnation and redemption,
the big themes played out in endless space. I had the vertiginous
sensation of leaning out over an abyss and peering downwards
into a colossal emptiness.

'This is your last chance. We're going.'

'You go. Go on. I'll catch up with you.'

If Hell itself had opened before me I could not have left
my seat. Margarete, seduced and betrayed, gave herself up to
God as Mephistopheles' giant black horses galloped away into
darkness. The audience exploded with joy and we were once
more in the human world of programmes and last trains home.
I fled from the balcony, hurtled down the bare staircases,
banged through the fire door and out into the night.

It was snowing.

East Berlin was still battered and morose, but now it
glittered, edged with bright crystals. The ice crust broke
beneath me and I left long tracks in the untouched white as I
flung myself down the streets, now unrecognisable, peering
into the white curtains of falling snow which masked the dark.
All the buildings close to the Wall were boarded up, unoccupied.
There were no streetlights, no cars, no people. I was terrified
and desperate. I no longer knew where I was going. No one
had followed me out into the white night. They were all
going the other way, streaming out of the theatre towards the
S-Bahn, back into the city, away from the Wall. The Wall was
dangerous dead space, even more sinister after dark.

I reached the Wall, shaken and shrunken with cold, at fifteen minutes to midnight. Here were the pools of yellow light, the ravelled expanses of barbed wire, the guard posts. I saw no soldiers on duty. The Wall was a stage set for murder, but nothing doing. I burst into a small Nissen hut. Here were two East German border guards, huddled round a stove; they were young, surprised and heavily armed. I stood, white and gasping, covered in wet snow, as they stamped my passport.

'The Wall's not shut. You can go over.'

It was ten minutes to twelve. I stepped out of the hut and into the silent, white world. The snow was still falling, now sparse and soft. The floodlights marked out the frontier. I could see the Wall, whitened, beautiful, stretching away into an infinite white. But the road across which we had sauntered that morning had now vanished. All before me lay untrodden space. The markers had gone.

I stood still, unable to go forwards or back.

I banged on the door of the hut. The soldiers looked out, hatless, puzzled.

'I can't do it. I'm too scared.'

We all stood there, baffled and confused, in the eerie yellow lights and great descending flakes of snow. Then one of the soldiers seized his rifle and his helmet.

'*Ruf doch mal die Amerikaner an. Wir bringen sie 'rüber mit.*' Call the Yanks. We'll take her over.

The other soldier picked up the phone and spoke in faultless English with a slight accent.

'Hello there. We're bringing one over. Meet us in the middle.'

They had a direct line.

106

Patricia Duncker

As we stepped forwards into the white night I huddled between my two guards who now wore massive military coats, shouldered their rifles and assumed a brisk parade-ground pace, chins up, boots kicking snow into clouds. We saw two shadows leaving the hut on the opposite side of Checkpoint Charlie. They were still pulling on their helmets and coats, getting dressed for the performance. Then they wheeled around, stiffened and began to march towards us. As their faces loomed out of the spectral mass of snow I saw their broad cheerful grins. For a moment we all fused into one group, stamped and saluted, and I was passed back from East to West, chilled and trembling.

But I wasn't the only thing that changed hands. There was a rapid muttering, an opening of great coats and a swift exchange of vodka and Russian belts, decorated with large red stars, swapped for girlie magazines, cigarettes, chocolate and oranges. Then all four saluted again with much shouldering of rifles and military clicks, swivelled about and marched back to their respective huts, each covered in an identical layer of crisp white snow. The red and white barriers descended and the Wall closed. It was midnight.

Those who actually live on a violent border, as the Wall once was, do well to speak each other's language. The soldiers who swept me across the Wall on that snowy night not only understood one another – they were friends. As a woman I have no country, and unlike Virginia Woolf, I do not presume to occupy the whole world. As a writer I have no country, my country is the English language. That language, which for me is something rich and strange, is the place where I am not a stranger, a foreigner or someone on a visit. It is home.

But in Wales, English is both a national language and a disputed terrain of vested interests, passionate attachments and irrational angers. Welsh is a language that has survived despite constant menace and outright attack; for me it is someone else's mother country, the place where they too feel at home. This is not a debate in which I can intervene; but nor is it a conflict I can ignore. English is an empire language, with an ambiguous, cruel history; but all languages, and all peoples, have dark uneasy pasts, if you take the trouble to dig. Shift the terms of the debate. How does Welsh speak to my other languages, the languages that are not English? How does Welsh speak to French, and above all, to German? For English is not my only language, although it is the most intimate of the languages I can speak and write, the one I wear closest to my skin. It is the language I use to interrogate, challenge, and describe the world. Most people speak more than one language or can negotiate complex relationships in a language that is not their mother tongue. I have heard Welsh spoken with energy and gusto in upstate New York and been thankful for the existence of basic Internet English in a remote corner of North Africa. A language may offer the security of a strong identity, but it also reaches across borders, frontiers and walls. One of the *langue d'Oc* language activists I met at a fête in Gaillac laid out his range of slogans before me. The one I chose to stick on my car read: *He who loses his language loses his country*.

German was the first language I learned that was not my mother tongue. It was the first language through which I learned to love another country, and it is a language whose past is both monstrous and rich with wonders. My German teacher was called George and I first encountered the Berlin

Patricia Duncker

Wall in George's classroom. The year must have been 1965 and Berlin was associated in my mind with Christopher Isherwood, Sally Bowles and a subsequent airlift of uncertain date. In fact, the Wall was then a relatively recent phenomenon, which, unbeknown to us, was exercising George's imagination. He sought out writing that mentioned the Wall and gave us short passages to translate. The most intriguing of these was from a novel by John Le Carré, the title of which, *Der Spion, der aus der Kälte hereinkam*, gave us some anxious moments, when we tackled it in twos. George gave me an approving tick in the margin of my exercise book and pointed out, for one of us had got it wrong, that it made no sense to write *hinein* or *hinaus*. The interesting implication in my German construction (*hereinkam*) was that whoever had called the spy in from the cold was already sitting there, comfortably, in the warm. George often gave us paragraphs from action-thrillers to translate, as we scampered towards O-Level, flicking through our dictionaries in an attempt to solve problems presented by Conan Doyle and Ian Fleming. George observed that the efficiency of a well-written sentence in an action narrative depended upon the correct use of good, strong, well-muscled verbs.

The Spy Who Came In From The Cold (1963) has an ingenious and spectacularly clever plot. It begins and ends, using some far from specious coincidences, but working towards a bitter, inevitable sense of closure, on the Berlin Wall. In the beginning, Alec Leamas, the burnt-out spy, watches his best East German agent, who has been betrayed and is on the run, gunned down by the frontier guards as he attempts to cycle across the border.

There was only one light in the checkpoint, a reading lamp with a green shade, but the glow of the arclights, like artificial moonlight, filled the cabin. Darkness had fallen and with it silence. They spoke as if they were afraid of being overheard. Leamas went to the window and waited, in front of him the road and to either side the Wall, a dirty ugly thing of breeze blocks and strands of barbed wire, lit with cheap yellow light, like the backdrop for a concentration camp. East and West of the Wall lay the unrestored part of Berlin, a half-world of ruin, drawn in two dimensions, crags of war.

This was the first description I ever read of the Wall, which was to become so potent a symbol in the Le Carré novels and so critical a presence in my own life. This was exactly how I perceived the Wall when I first set eyes upon it and how I remember the thing, even now, when I have watched it hacked to bits, in the process of vanishing. Le Carré exactly catches the theatricality of the Wall. It is an empty stage set, waiting for history to happen. He describes the entire scene in terms of light: the reading lamp, the arclights, the cheap yellow neon, which illuminates the Wall. It is also a relic of the war, a link with Germany's monstrous past, turning the Eastern Zone into one vast concentration camp. The Wall is a place of paralysis, where time stops, extends, where the two minutes you have been given to get over turn into an entire chapter, page after page in the book. Le Carré's spies, all through his novels, wait patiently, anxiously, at the Wall. When you reach the edge of the Zone, all you can do is stand at the Wall and wait.

In the final scene of the book, Leamas refuses to abandon the body of his one-time lover, a very silly woman, who has just been shot dead while scaling the Wall, and he too is finally shot. Our hero and somewhat qualified heroine both go down in a hail of bullets. We, the schoolchildren, busy with our translations, all liked the book, but not for its disillusioned, embittered and weary hero, and especially not for the woman, Liz Gold, a sentimental, credulous and colourless character who was peculiarly easy to seduce. Why she had joined the Communist Party and taken to selling the *Daily Worker* rather than joining the Church and concentrating on marketing the parish magazine, was beyond us. She was clearly one of those perpetual, self-sacrificing victims, who needed to belong to something or someone, preferably a man, to give her shape and form. She was the woman we had been told never to be. In my case, she was the woman my mother had warned me about. Never become her, and never be her friend.

As I read John Le Carré's novels from time to time over the next forty years, I realised that this feminine pattern never changed. Women are formless, meaningless, a sort of undisciplined swamp of emotions, who need men, or men's institutions to give them shape, structure and purpose. Ann Smiley is an implausible middle-aged nymphomaniac, fond of having sex with younger men, whom we never see her actually seducing. By the time we get to *Smiley's People* she is rapidly reaching her sell-by date. Ann has the decency to remain largely off-stage. Peter Guillam's flute-playing Camilla in *Tinker, Tailor, Soldier, Spy* (1974) is a dry run, twenty years in advance, for the equally ambiguous, mysterious, young, musical Emma in *Our Game* (1994). Even the prodigious Connie, the retired ex-Moscow watcher from the 'Smiley' novels, who I hoped might break the mould, is an amorphous mass of alcoholic memories, a catalogue of Moscow hoods, a heap of shapeless scraps of information. Only George Smiley has the key to their significance. Connie can never face up to things. If the game is turning nasty among her 'lovely boys', she doesn't want to know, especially not who the mole is. Connie is too old, too ugly and too queer to be a serious sexual proposition. The sexually willing girls, and they are silly girls, every single one of them, actually wait naked at windows for the retired, middle-aged spies to get home. But Le Carré's books aren't about these naïve, credulous women, who can, nevertheless, be instrumental in the plots. His books are all about men.

The tales in the Le Carré canon are about honour, betrayal, friendship, trust and relationships between men. And it was this that we, as schoolchildren, loved about his novels. These are all English schoolboy values. They were our values. We liked them for that very reason. And we saw clearly that the Wall was the place where you made choices – either/or. It was a dangerous dividing line and to cross it involved a great risk. But the moment of crossing was also the moment of proving your treachery or integrity. As Leamas does when he chooses to die rather than continue his profession of betrayal.

The naïve, spineless or sex-obsessed women in Le Carré's novels seemed contemptible because they were unable to carve out a shape or an identity for themselves without becoming part of a larger group or falling in love with a man. They could not become heroines because they did not choose that radical independence which is the basis of all freedom. Even in largely white Western Europe, a very small corner of this world, few women travel alone. When I am driving through Britain on the great roads I count how many women I can spot travelling alone. There are never more than five or six. You see them in towns, going to work, shopping or collecting their children. Women use public transport more than men do. We are poorer than men, we don't all own cars. But, on the whole, when I travel through Europe, as a woman alone, I rarely see other women unaccompanied. And the only women alone I have ever met in the riskier parts of the world are intrepid backpacking Australians or New Zealanders who erupt with rage like hot geysers when they describe the incessant sexual harassment they have encountered from almost every man they met en route. My guides, all men, are incredulous. If you are a woman travelling alone you are simply asking for it. Why can't you understand that? Well, I can't and I won't, because I will not accept that women are not free to go where they will, whenever they want to do so.

I don't think that it is possible to be a writer if you do not have a powerful sense of your own boundaries, both the limits and the edges of the self. These are your own walls, for which every woman especially is responsible. They are exceedingly hard to build. For women this means claiming that radical independence which I experience as a rich privilege, and Virginia Woolf described as five hundred a year, now around twenty-five grand, and a room of one's own. Independence can be measured in terms of space, money, time. But it is also the courage to cross all the walls and borders, learn a new language, and leave home. So many fictional heroines are supposedly in search of a safe place in which they can find love, children, a community and a secure future. One of the great recurring clichés in contemporary women's fiction is that tension evident in the desire for radical independence and yet the need to remain within the relative safety of home. We are told to stay home because if we do we can be locked in, tied down or otherwise constrained. But home is not a safe place and there is no such thing as safety. In any case, safety does not come first.

Leave home.

All our cultural and ideological influences are pushing us to make a different decision, to stifle our desire for adventure and to put the comfort and happiness of everyone else before our own. Even a childless, single woman like Le Carré's hapless Liz Gold feels obliged to dedicate her life to the greater cause of Communism. What makes her so dependent and compliant? The fear of loneliness? Of not being able to manage? Or has she just succumbed to some very effective brainwashing? I know that few women have sufficient access to money, space and time to make any substantial change to the lives they have inherited. But why is that? Why are we kept poor, illiterate, limited in our knowledge and our expectations? And by whom? Why is travelling alone a risky thing to do? Who harasses you when you undertake your great voyages, and makes your life hell?

Where is the virtue in belonging? A greater freedom lies in not belonging. I cannot forget that production of *Faust* in East Berlin. It was a classic case of evading the censor and addressing the unconscious of the audience. I heard what that production was telling me that night and I still treasure the insight. We all have the right to be unsatisfied, to refuse to belong, to want more, more of everything, to leave home and live at risk. We can cross all the Walls, or rip them down.

A happy end is not usually a boundless highway with no conclusion to the journey ever mooted or described. Those are men's dreams, the journey without end. But that is what I choose, and I prefer to travel at night.

Even the radio sputters and fades into static as I cross the Plynlimon range. There is ice on the road, slow down. The sign says MOUNTAIN LAMBS ARE SWEETER. More adorable, or more delicious? Or both? Then, unaccountably, the rocks before me proclaim ELVIS LIVES. It is now nearly two in the morning. I climb past the Red Kite visitor's centre and I know that beyond the dark folds of those cunning hills there is nothing left except the sea. I perch on the edge of Wales, the boundary of Britain, the rim of Europe. The descent begins. No lights in the valley and no traffic. The last car I saw was at Llangurig. Aberystwyth curls around the bay, folded in silence and sleep. I slow right down, dip my lights and creep back along North Road, towards the sleeping house.

My cousin comes from Kinross in Scotland where my father's brother ended up, thousands of miles away from his own country, running a garage. He married a Scottish girl and settled down. Marion Rose spent part of her life in Mozambique. Why, I asked, did you go back to Scotland? And this was her answer. 'I didn't want to be a foreigner forever.' So she went back to the country where she was born, to her hills and lochs, to the people who spoke with her accent. She went home. I do not have that choice. I have become *l'étrangère, die Fremde*, an incomer, a person who is not from this place, whatever the place, a foreigner forever. And here are some of the things I have learned. Try to live lightly in a country that is not your own. Listen more than you speak and never imagine that your roots are permanent. Be unobtrusive. Be quiet. Leave no messages, no trace. Keep the car running, fuelled, packed, and be ready to move. Wait for the dark.

Notes

Teithio yn y Nos/Nachtreise – night journey

The Splinter of Ice

Liz Jones

When I found the eviction notice pinned to my front door,
I could feel something move inside me, something other than
the baby in my womb. It felt like my life, backing up and
changing direction. I had spent my pregnancy in a dream. If
I had thought about the future at all, I had imagined that
our happy, disorganised life would just carry on – the only
difference, there'd be three of us, instead of two. Now, as I
tried to decipher the small print on a Notice to Quit, I felt an
icy hand on my shoulder. In two weeks, I was to have a baby
and we – mother, father and baby – were to be homeless. That
moment was to change me, turn me into a rainy-day saver,
peeping round corners, always on the lookout for danger
ahead. The sky had turned dark and I'd wandered into the
frozen wastes. I didn't know it then, but a splinter of ice had
lodged itself in my heart.

This was during the reign of Margaret Thatcher, that Snow Queen made flesh, at a time when she seemed almost indestructible. Our landlords, a London Labour-controlled council, had neglected to renew our short-term tenancy. They'd also neglected to tell us that they were selling our home over our heads, as part of a 'portfolio' of properties, to private developers. The Snow Queen was advancing, freezing the hearts of her old political enemies.

Anyone who's sat in a waiting room of a council homeless people's unit with a child or a swelling pregnant belly, will know the gnawing, powerless anxiety that can turn a person's hair white overnight. Anyone who's been humiliated by a judge for being homeless and desperate will have felt their life career out of control, will know how a wry 'I'm sorry, Miss Jones, but we can't offer you the Ritz' (that one really raised a laugh in the court) can turn a person into a clown, one of the comic poor. Anyone who's been through it would swear to do everything in their power, sell their soul if necessary, so long as it meant never having to face that humiliation again.

We were relieved to have found a housing association flat. Feeling grateful that our baby wasn't to begin life in a bed and breakfast, we resolved to live in a shrunken world, to give up our dreamy indigence. Simon left art college and found a job; I gave up writing unprofitably for radical magazines and together we set about our new, fearful life. My spirit crushed, my ideals defeated, now all I had was my little family and my new quest for security. I didn't know it, but the ice-splinter was growing. When Sian was six months old, I found work as a housing officer with a London council (not our old landlords) – employers who were generous enough to treat my experience of homelessness as a transferable skill. It was straightforward enough, preparing to be a working mother – before I'd felt the pain and guilt that goes with it. I had no problem with the idea of working mothers; far from it. I thought of myself as a feminist – I still do – and didn't have much time for traditional gender roles. I knew in advance that looking after a baby was an exhausting, relentless business; that going out to work had to be better than a day spent changing nappies and mopping baby food off the floor. What feminism hadn't prepared me for, though, was the overwhelming love I was to feel for my baby. Those sublime mother-and-baby moments, the heart-stopping smiles and gurgles that were to play havoc with my postnatal hormones. That was when a voice would whisper, beg me not to do it – not to leave her. Then another voice – a loud, strident one – would interrupt, order me to go out and earn money, save up, buy a house, don't get left behind. After all, everyone else is doing it – it's what a family has to do. Toughen up, it said, keep on working. I gave the voice a name – I called it Financial Security. Now I know it was the Snow Queen talking.

We were living now in Bethnal Green on the edge of the booming City of London. At night, we would gaze through our window at its empty ice palaces – the Nat West Tower, the brand new Lloyds Building – glittering in the darkness like the Northern Lights. Our neighbourhood was mostly a mix of white Eastenders and immigrants from Bangladesh. It was a poor area – a lot of our neighbours were living on the edge, struggling to get by. It was the kind of place where mothers of young children stayed at home, not because they chose to, but because they couldn't earn enough to pay for childcare. It seemed as though I was doing the opposite – going out to work because I felt I had no choice. Before my job had started, I would watch the full-time mothers with their children – down the shops, in the park, sometimes with grandmothers and sisters, nephews and nieces in tow – and feel shot through with grief for what I was about to lose.

Then there were the creatives – artists, writers, musicians who were moving in and converting dank old warehouses into rambling family homes. I knew a few of them; they seemed to thrive on parenthood – for them child-rearing was part of their expressive, spontaneous lifestyle. How I envied them. I envied what I saw as their easier, happier lives; the way they filled their days with a cheerful mish-mash of self-styled Steiner playgroups, outings to city farms and summer bolt-holes in Picardy or Benbecula. To them, motherhood was the warm, nurturing, expansive business that I longed for it to be.

There were plenty of people like us, too – the near-invisible office drones burrowing away by day in our air-conditioned warrens, scurrying home in darkness, stopping only to gather up children and shopping. As Thatcherism was punishing the poor and the weak, those of us who had a foothold in what passed as the middle class couldn't take it for granted – we had to fight to stay there, be vigilant against slipping and falling down into the underclass. We had to put our work before anything, even our own children. Simon and I hadn't just become dual working parents – we had sleepwalked into a new social phenomenon. Nine to five was no longer enough – we had to love our work, take it home, tend to it evenings and weekends, as if it would wilt and die if neglected out of hours. No matter what I was doing – reading Sian a bedtime story, playing a bathtime game, flopping in front of *Hill Street Blues*, picking at a supper of cold pasta – my mental in-tray was always with me. Women like me – mothers of children under five – were entering and re-entering the workforce in our droves. Most of us had no choice – especially if we were living in London or south-east England, where property prices were spiralling. And – the unkindest cut – this was happening at a time when work was changing; when the workplace was getting tougher and meaner. Add to that the dearth of decent, affordable childcare – the few subsidised nurseries there were couldn't begin to meet this unprecedented demand. The tardy offer of a place at our local council nursery, just one week before Sian was due to start school, wasn't at all unusual. The Snow Queen had consulted her Mirror of Wisdom, the only one, the best in the world, the one that told her that the market was the answer. There would be no extra money – free enterprise will meet the demand, create private nurseries across the land. Meanwhile, childcare in the private sector was patchy, unpredictable and sometimes downright seedy. The better-off had to go and find a good nanny, while we had to look for a childminder or a 'budget' private nursery. As the search began, my heart was freezing over, numbing the painful thought of leaving my child with some as-yet-unknown person before either of us was ready.

When I managed to find a private nursery – one that involved a relatively short ninety-minute round trip – I was delighted. At £100 a week it was more than we could afford, but it seemed caring, professionally run, worth every penny. The publicity material was impressive too – glossy brochures with pictures of beaming infants playing in a sunny room with French windows, 'a stimulating, creative environment' which provided the 'highest standards of childcare'. The nursery was indeed as bright and sunny as the brochure suggested.

But the French windows – which opened out onto a yard patrolled by forklift trucks – had to be kept permanently locked, starving the overheated room of fresh air. Leaving Sian there for her two-hour 'settling in' session was difficult. She had never in her six-month life been cared for by anyone other than Simon or me. But Amy, the business-suited proprietor – and, as the brochure had informed us, mother of a two-year-old boy who loved to go to the nursery – was a model of calm and reassurance.

'Don't worry,' she said, 'your daughter will be fine.' Two hours later, I returned to find Sian in the corner, strapped up in a baby chair, convulsed with sobs. A teenage girl, the only member of staff on duty, had literally turned her back on Sian and was occupying herself with a happier-looking baby. I marched up the stairs to Amy's office, trying to console Sian, who was drenched in snot and tears and still wailing. Amy shrugged.

'It happens sometimes,' she said, wrapping her arm protectively around her own little boy. A couple of weeks later, I was to see Amy again – as a talking head in a TV commercial (her husband worked in advertising). 'As a mother and a nursery manager,' she said, a little nervous, but warming to the camera, 'I like nothing better than to see my children happy. That's why I always use XX nappies.' I suppose I should have complained, blown the whistle, but there was no time – I was starting work in less than two weeks and was trawling through the social services list of registered childminders, a task that was fast becoming a full-scale campaign. In any case, I reasoned, complaining wouldn't change anything – it was legal enough to run a shoddy, cut-price nursery where babies are allowed to cry, so long as they're supervised and don't break any bones.

Liz Jones

It was a funny business, this quest for the ideal substitute mother – and not helped at all by the myths that were doing the rounds of anxious mothers. You rarely heard about the 'good enough' childminder, who was fine but not perfect. Like the mothers in fairy tales, the childminder was always an archetype – a monster or a madonna. There was the wicked childminder who neglected her charges, dumped them in front of the telly all day, or even outside in the pram. Then, the greatest fear of all, the monster that stalked every mother's worst nightmare – the child abuser. The good childminder was an angel, fairy godmother and household goddess all rolled into one. She could be a worry too – invoking as she did that other fear that gnaws at the working mother – the fear that says what if my child loves *her* more than she loves me. I needn't have worried: the good-enough was evading me, and I was beginning to doubt if the perfect one existed at all.

Unable to find anyone suitable through Social Services, we put an advertisement in the newsagent's window for a 'Caring childminder for our lovely daughter'. A perfectly normal business transaction, said my ice-cold heart. Yet it felt wrong – at least the Social Services' register was regulated and involved people who actively wanted to be childminders, had gone through the registration process and maybe some formal training. Advertising felt cheap – like we were putting our child up for sale. It was also to throw up a dispiriting selection of candidates, all different, but sharing one feature in common – an innate lack of interest in anything to do with caring for children. There was the teenage girl who planned to pass Sian off as her own child and leave her in the college crèche; the doped-out Goth whose flat reeked of patchouli and

123

bin juice; the jolly-looking grandmother who volunteered that I wasn't to worry as she'd make sure my little girl didn't play with 'any of them Paki kids'.

We returned to the Social Services' register. This time, we were luckier. Marcia was a kind, softly spoken Jamaican woman and Sian took to her straight away. The only problem was the sandpit – or the lack of it. As working parents – and parents of an only child – guilt and anxiety made us willing to believe any new, faddish theory on child development. We had read somewhere – probably in a Sunday supplement – that a sandpit, above all other toys, was essential to a baby's intellectual and physical development, and had decided to buy one for Marcia, for Sian to use. Marcia declined our offer, quite reasonably, on the grounds that there was no room for a sandpit in her small, third-floor flat. Instead, she said she would take Sian, whenever she could, to the local parent-toddlers' group, which had an enormous sandpit. She must have regretted it, because from then on, whenever I called to pick up my daughter, I'd always get round to the same question – has Sian been in the sandpit today. After months of interrogation, Marcia cracked. I didn't catch the exact words muttered under her breath, but they sounded like 'I'm sick of that bloody sandpit'. A few days later, she told me she was giving up childminding to train to be a nursery nurse. It sounded like a good career move, and I even managed some encouraging noises, but inside I could feel the gut-wrenching panic returning. Weeks later, I saw Marcia in the street, pushing a double buggy. She nodded and crossed the road. Later, a neighbour let slip that Marcia hadn't gone to college, but had carried on childminding. My guilt-driven nagging and interfering had not only lost me a good childminder, it had turned an honest woman into a liar.

At twenty-one, Kathy, our next childminder, was young. But she did have two children of her own (one of them Sian's age) and she was warm and lively and a natural around children. We were lucky to find her, we decided, especially so soon after losing Marcia. Her husband, Dave, was a school caretaker – a job that came with a large house and garden, plenty of room for a toddler to play and explore. Sian got on well with all the family – Kathy, her children and Dave, who was always popping in and out during the day. For months, the arrangement seemed as close to perfect as it could get – until the morning when Sian cried all the way to Kathy's. After that, there were other mornings, plenty of them, when Sian didn't want to go. I was worried, but Kathy just laughed. Don't worry about it, she said, all kids go through a phase like that. In any case, Sian was always right as rain as soon as I'd gone. I chose to believe it. I had a future invested in believing it – we had just bought a house and we needed two incomes more than ever. Giving up my job wasn't an option. The prospect of losing our home was real and tangible; it had happened to us once and couldn't be brushed aside as something that only happened to other people. The fear of it blinded me, even to my child's unhappiness.

I knew something was up when I saw Kathy standing at the door waiting for me. Close up, I could see her bruised and swollen eye. Inside, Sian was huddled under the table, her face pale and screwed up with rage. I'll never know how long Dave had been violent, or how much of it Sian had seen. I only know that Sian had tried her best to tell me, but I wasn't listening. The splinter of ice had done its work.

I could make a case for my defence, say that I couldn't

have known, that I did my best. I could also say that I was driven by some misguided quest to rejoin society, to grab a handful of security through hard work and property ownership – a security which, looking back, was illusory and only created more insecurity; a security for which our little girl was to pay the price. Now, when I look at my beautiful, talented eighteen-year-old daughter, I'm amazed at how all that serenity and self-assurance could have sprung out of such confusion. But there have been times – rows, rebellions, the inevitable kicking against me – when I've remembered the splinter of ice and wondered, would she have been so angry with me if I hadn't left her with strangers. Sometimes, I still wonder why I let fear get the better of me, and couldn't feel it freezing my heart.

Chicken in a Basket

Catherine Johnson

When I started this I thought that what I wanted to write was a memoir of how I learned not to be Welsh. A two-thousand-word almost-truth about how I realised that I could never be Welsh even if my great great great Uncle was Twm o'r Nant and my cousin Gwyn had won the chair at the Eisteddfod. But I normally write fiction – a neat payoff, a truth realised within a few pages the way it never is in life. And in life my revelation took years, ten or fifteen at least. It's a mass of little things layered on top of each other: looks, words out of place, things which seem funny at first but which add up to the conclusion that – *you are not white*. And I'll never be white so I'll never be Welsh. It's that simple. But I didn't realise that when I was growing up.

What happened was this. The girl you're about to see, aged eleven, in the orchard of a derelict house near Gwytherin is wholly Welsh. She may live in London for forty-five weeks of the year and her father is Jamaican but she is Welsh. She is as Welsh and almost as black as the cattle lower down the valley. And she is one hundred and ten per cent sure of this. It's only later, slowly, slowly as she grows and the sideways looks get longer and London becomes safer and safer and more accepting that she realises she could never be Welsh. So I had wanted to write a story, which cleverly and completely encapsulated this. The transition from Welsh Jamaican to London through and through. But it didn't happen in one day, one night or one summer. And it would be a very dull read, being merely life, so this is just the story of one of those summers.

And this isn't exactly the truth. It's a kind of truth; my truth. Which I guarantee, is pretty elastic ropey old truth. All those books, all those chapters that start Training the Eye or Exploring Memory, they're never exact. Truth is what we make it. Like shining a torch around in a cellar. And the chicken in a basket is important because it's summer. Eating with your fingers, greasy salty hot food with no knives or forks.

So, why would I want to be Welsh? Well, we always went to Wales in the summer. A family of four travelling to Jamaica was completely out of the question. We couldn't afford it. Dad talked of Custard Apples and Sour Sop, and to us those words were more foreign than *hogen dda*[1], or *gwallt neis*[2]. And Wales was my mother's place, her home. She knew everyone, and everyone knew me. I felt I did belong – I was 'Rinwen's girl'. It only took one look at me, the only black girl in the village, to realise that.

It was 1973, the summer after I'd passed the entrance exam for a girls' grammar school. My parents only sent me for the exam because the headmaster of my primary school thought I was clever. When we went back to London and my friends were all off to the comprehensive down the road, I would be learning Latin and wearing a ridiculous school uniform with square-necked jumpers. I had tried to fail the exam – obviously not hard enough. But it was the start of my new relationship with exams; instead of always being top of the class I would now never again try hard enough.

My dad, like normal working people, barely had holidays – one week at the most. But my mum was a teacher, so the holidays were long. And my Nain and Taid lived in a small village, Llanfair Talhaearn, a few miles from the coast at Abergele. Theirs was a tiny cottage, three rooms and a chemical toilet up the hill. The height of luxury was the house across the road's outdoor flushing toilet. You could sneak in through the back gate. The woman that lived in the house had goitre. I didn't know that's what it was then. She had a huge neck that looked as if she'd swallowed a rugby ball. Fascinating. It wobbled as she spoke.

My grandparents' other neighbours were interesting too: a married couple with no children, up the hill in a kind of bright pastel painted bungalow. A married couple with no children. He drove around with a model fire extinguisher on his car to advertise his business. They had a big garage and a swing seat. I was never allowed on that swing seat. Now as an adult I manufacture lists of reasons for her hatred of children. It wasn't just me – back then, I just thought she was nuts. We weren't even allowed inside her house. You could stand on the step and smell the stillness in the air and see her collection of dolls lined up in glass cabinets.

We stayed in a blue and cream caravan up in the garden under the apple trees. The beds had candlewick covers and it smelled of damp. You could look out of the window and see the whole village down in the valley below. Across to the church and the many chapels, the silver metal strip of river, the curved stone bridge and the two pubs.

So this particular summer, my mother had seen a house, Hafod Bach, a ruined, almost but not quite derelict house a mile or so outside the village, Gwytherin, where she was born. No one wanted to live up there. In those days it would take forever just to drive to the coast road. There was no commuting to jobs in Chester, no European-funded glass factory in St Asaph. Even the village pub tried everything to get punters in, including keeping lions, real live lions – but they didn't last long. Gwytherin was much bleaker, less picture-book than Llanfair Talhaearn, and further up towards the moors. It was one of the last villages before Mynydd Hiraethog. It was so remote that everyone spoke Welsh, even Mr Malletan and he was German.

Hafod Bach was high up and the orchard held a few wind-whipped fruit trees. There were no flowers. Well maybe tiny ones – some dark blue *llus* in the hedges at the end of summer. But mostly just that grey-green mountain grass, those clumps of reeds you could make candles out of, and the odd spray of rusty bracken. The house was empty, almost derelict and full of owl pellets. I can remember turning one over, poking it with a stick, finding tiny dull-white mouse leg bones. Thinking about it now, it was the last place on earth you'd want a holiday home. Alone on the ridge of a hill, listening to the wind at night; no streetlights, no neighbours, miles from anywhere and the lanes full of ghosts.

But Mum wanted to buy it, and it was very cheap. I loved the idea too: I thought I was a country girl. I was already imagining my own pony in the orchard. It would be our country house and maybe it would be mine one day. After all I would leave London when I grew up, and live here permanently, wouldn't I? We weren't rich, Dad was a tailor, we lived in suburban London and owned a Morris Thousand Traveller. The whole idea, I can see now, was mad.

But the rest of the summer ploughed along as usual. Except for me there was the dread of the new school. Full of people I didn't know, the start of the rest of my life. I always imagined then, that I would grow up and live in Wales. In the country that I loved and that loved me back. The house seemed a step closer to that. I'd have my own home with my horse and I was sure in my Welshness then. London was just the place I lived in during the gaps between the summer holidays. My Welshness became just another excuse for my sense of being different I suppose.

Of course holiday homes, English holiday homes, were a bad thing. But we weren't English, whichever way you looked at it. My dad was Jamaican, which was, of course, a million million times better than being English. In our house the English were always the oppressors, whether you were talking about the version of Paul Bogle and the Morant Bay uprising or Saunders Lewis, whether you were peasants or slaves. And even though I was born in England and went to school there, I knew it would be stupid to call myself English. Other English people would look at me and laugh – 'No, where are you from, where are you *really* from?'

Of course I know now that the Welsh, or for that matter the Jamaicans, aren't any different. They can tell by the colour of my skin or the way I speak that I'm an outsider. The only place I truly belong is London where our graffiti reads *Half Caste Power!* and it's not being ironic.

Hafod Bach wouldn't be a mere English holiday cottage, just tinder for the language society. Or at least it wouldn't be once we'd bought it. We were family; our roots went deep into the soil.

The house was on land that belonged to a second or third cousin. Everyone was related – no really they were: my Taid could name every family in every farm on the way down to Llanrwst or the other way to Pentrefoelas – and this cousin was called William. I couldn't tell you his last name but I'd put money on it being Williams or Roberts. His first name was shortened to Cwil. It was all sorted. My mum and me went to see him. We needed things signed.

Cwil's yard was like this: an orange-chestnut colt with a head-collar tied with blue baler twine to a post, hens with bright red combs, yellow beaks. Black and white dogs chained up, barking, three or four dogs, one with a milky blue wall eye. Nel or Mot, I suppose. The noise of the chains grating against the corrugated-iron dog houses, the summer trees still bright green. The light shining through in bright clear patches. That noise of crows calling high up.

Cwil didn't speak English. There weren't many left in my family who didn't. Even my Nain managed sentences – *Make your hair!* and the like – but she had grown up when you didn't need the language. When she was my age – no, younger – she'd been employed to fill a gap in the hedge to stop sheep getting out.

Cwil had an ancient Welsh cliché of a face. Think of the halfwit who isn't a halfwit in Alan Garner's *The Owl Service*. Big features, dark eyes. I stayed in the yard while my mum went into the farmhouse. Tried to make friends with the orange colt by blowing gently up its nostrils – that's what you

do with horses. Chased the hens, and stayed just far enough
away from the dogs.

I was waiting in the yard a long time. In one of the outhouses
on a window ledge was a tiny green glass bottle. There were
cobwebs and everything seemed broken. I thought it funny,
a grown man living in all this space on his own. Only old
people lived alone.

When Mum came out of the house she was on the point
of crying. She held it long enough to walk back to the car
and drive out into the high-sided lane. He had changed his
mind, just like that. He wasn't selling. I don't remember how
she drove back to Llanfair Talhaearn but she must have. I
think I was crying too. Something had changed his mind. I
imagined him looking out of his kitchen window and seeing
me trying to befriend his colt or chase his chickens. When you
are a child the world revolves around you. I was sure something about me had changed his mind. The way I worried his
hens. The way I'd tickled the colt's neck or blown up its shell-
like pink nostrils. The way I looked. Whatever. He had decided
not to sell.

We must have stopped at the Swan Inn in Llanfair
Talhaearn to console ourselves with chicken in the basket.
There were real baskets then, not imitation basket-look
plastic.

My mother put on a brave face. She didn't really do
complaining. She just said there must be a reason and we
never really talked about it. I didn't anyway. That was that. No
more holiday home ever. We couldn't really afford it anyway.
It was a silly idea and the house was near where she'd seen a
ghost as a child. She said she was walking to catch the school

bus when she saw him, looking along the road to Pandy Tudur dressed for 1940s Hollywood in a trench coat and trilby. As far as she knew he was probably still there, drifting between the bracken and cow parsley hedgerows waiting for someone like Hedy Lamarr.

When I drove past the house this summer Hafod Bach was still there. The house is still empty. There's no roof now and the trees are dead, strangled with lichen and scorched by wind. Cwil has been dead a long time. He never did sell it. It stayed empty and now it's no good even for owls. I showed my son the house when we were there at Whitsun. I think he thought we must have been mad.

And I would never call myself Welsh now; I mean how stupid is that! Look at me – no, go on, have a good look. Do I look Welsh to you?

Notes

[1] *Hogen dda* – good girl
[2] *Gwallt neis* – nice hair

The Morant Bay uprising against ill-treatment of freed slaves is a seminal event in Jamaican national history. Paul Bogle, whose petition sparked it, was hanged and is still today a Jamaican national hero.

Me and My Welsh Hat

Caryl Lewis

My grandmother was a farm labourer by the age of fourteen. She received limited schooling (only the brightest boys in the family were given an education) and was married to a farmer by eighteen. Today I'm sitting in the same *milltir sgwâr*[1] trying to eke out a living from the same beautiful but unforgiving landscape. At the risk of sounding 'Heaney-esque', she used her hands whilst I'm trying to use a pen. I'm really not too sure yet which will prove more successful.

When I was a child of about five, I remember sitting in the horseshoe of my grandmother's lap. It was a sunny day, bright with light and as we sat in the garden, we could hear the men bringing in the hay from the fields nearby. She had stolen out with me for a few quiet minutes' break between spreading the table with a veritable banquet of cold hams, salads from the garden and jelly and ice-cream and going back to work. She knew that after lunch, she would take me in the pram and leave me by the hedge of the field as she carried hay bales with the rest of the men. I held her hands that day and marvelled at their smoothness. Their marble-like nothingness. Holding her thick fingers in mine, I wondered where her prints had gone, where her grip had disappeared to. I even sang about her *bysedd cerrig-mor* – her sea-stone fingers. When I asked her about it, she smiled, before replying, 'It's hard work being a Welsh woman.' As I lay in bed that night, the *carthen*[2] bound tightly around me, the pitch darkness and clean-shaven fields breathing outside the window, I felt troubled by her words. I remember deciding that if being a Welsh woman was such hard work, then I'd have to grow up to be Japanese or even an American cow-girl, like I'd seen in the films. What I couldn't fathom at that age of course, was why she smiled when she said it. Hard work for me later would be English grammar, which seemed so alien compared to the Welsh one. That was certainly nothing to smile about. What I realise now is that although her identity had all but been erased by her living in that landscape, she never looked more powerful and happy as when she sat there, sharing a stolen moment with her grand-daughter. The disappearance of her identity seemed to signal her diffusion into, and union with her life, rather than her subjugation to it.

This was my first encounter with my own culture. Like coming across yourself in a mirror for the first time. I suddenly had the sense that there was something of the 'other' about me. Until then, my culture was something natural, unconscious like water and air. As I grew, these encounters became more frequent and as it dawned on me that not everyone in the world spoke Welsh, and that becoming Japanese wasn't really an option, then I'd have to come to terms with it. Whatever *it* was. This loss of an unconscious cultural identity seems much more acute when living within a minority sub-culture, and once this 'deflowering' has occurred, it is a question of feeling your way towards a sense of your own 'Welshness'. It is this search for a sense of 'Welshness' and a sense of place that now informs my work as a writer and I struggle daily between living naturally and obliviously in an entirely Welsh environment one minute, and being painfully aware of my Welshness the next.

My next encounter with this 'otherness' came, like to many young Welsh girls, on St David's Day at primary school. All the children would put on traditional dress in order to attend school that day. We'd then have Welsh cakes and cawl and we'd have games instead of lessons. There was one catch though. Like all Welsh children I had seen the painting *Salem*, the most iconic image of the Welsh woman in Welsh art history. My grandmother had a copy on a calendar and my other grandmother had a picture of it in a book she kept under her sewing box. In it, a dour-faced old Welsh woman in traditional dress arrives late for chapel. Her tardiness is intentional as she is wearing a new shawl and is keen that everyone look at her so that she may show it off. She is punished for her vanity and wickedness very publicly when the face of the devil is seen in the folds of her new shawl. The 'witchiness' of her hat and the devil in her shawl had filled my bad dreams as had the cowed and bowed heads of some of the other worshippers in the chapel. It was no wonder then, when St David's Day came around, that I had certain reservations about wearing clothes like hers. I also remember thinking that if this was what 'proper' Welsh women wore every day, then I certainly wasn't Welsh. I didn't even know anyone who was

Welsh. Perhaps, I thought, there was another country where proper Welsh women lived. Some of the other kids, mostly ones from English or mixed backgrounds, got away with wearing jeans and a Welsh rugby shirt and suddenly I realised that that's what I wanted to wear. I became convinced that I wasn't Welsh, and that there was a remote possibility that I might even be English....

Anyway, every year, we were paraded through town, a bell ringing so that everyone could come out to see us. Every year there was a prize for the best costume and every year, the thick woollen tights I wore would sag between my knees, forcing me into an undignified near-waddle. I didn't know how those Welsh ladies did it. That year, the excitement of the day, the countless Welsh cakes and bowlfuls of cawl took their toll and culminated in, to my eternal shame, my throwing up in my Welsh hat. The felt became soggy and misshapen and I still, even today, flush red at that sacrilege. I stood, holding my hat still full of sick, looking up at the pictures of those immaculate Welsh ladies, their angular hats sloping elegantly around their very particular-looking faces, feeling that even if I tried really hard, I'd never be good enough to be a proper Welsh lady.

My relationship with this iconic image of the Welsh woman somehow continued through my teens. My mother, a singer, would sometimes don the apparel for special appearances or concerts. (There was also the time when she was almost flung into a Kuwaiti jail for trying to smuggle a pork pie into the country in her Welsh hat for some poor non-Muslim who was suffering severely from a fifteen-year pork drought, but that's another story). I spent my early teens either at home with my grandparents or trailing her around backstage carrying her guitar case. We travelled the length and breadth of Wales, my father setting up sound systems and generally making sure everything was alright. There wasn't a chippy or late-night garage with toilets that we didn't know about.

I learnt that this image of the Welsh woman was marketable, covetable even and most definitely entertaining. I learnt that Americans would give you twenty-pound notes for standing on a chair and giving a half-decent rendition of *Dau Gi Bach yn Mynd i'r Coed* [3] but still the whole thing troubled me, as it troubled my mother. My mother was a splendid Welsh woman and so much more appealing than what this costume seemed to represent. It had a feel-good factor that seemed to work on everyone except us. Sadly, it was what they wanted to see. I shall never forget sitting backstage, eating crisps and watching my mother get ready for a big St David's Day concert. I watched her unfolding her costume gently before dressing, smoothing away creases slowly with the palms of her hands. I instinctively knew not to talk and babble on before a performance; I must have sensed that she was preparing everything in her head. I'd watch as she put on her stage make-up thickly, her blusher making her look as if she had two lives in her. She looked quite beautiful as she placed the hat on her head and took her guitar to go on stage. Whilst she was on, my father and I used to chat or he'd sneak me some chocolate. We'd never listen. It made us too nervous. Afterwards, she'd come off stage relieved and energised from the performance. She was never tired, she was always buzzing, but every time she changed back to her everyday clothes almost immediately. Taking off her hat, she would brush it as if trying to cleanse it from the vulgarity of the bright lights and the cheers; she'd shake the taint of the 'popular appeal' out of her skirt like dust and put everything away as if it was precious. She was right: it never looked right out there somehow, but she did it, because it raised the profile of Welshness and challenged some peoples' perceptions as much as it reinforced other stereotypes.

Like many of my friends, I decided to leave for England for University. We weren't running away. We were just looking for something different. A chance perhaps to live somewhere where nobody knew you. To be able to go to the pub in the afternoon and not have it reported back to your mother and grandmother! Ironically, the night I landed in my new student block, I opened the door to find I'd been placed with another, non-Welsh-speaking, girl from Wales, a token Irish student and a couple of black guys. We were making up the minority statistics and perhaps they thought we'd be more comfortable together. Which, perhaps, we were. It was a strange experience. For the first time in my life I had to speak English every day. It was genuinely tiring and at the end of the day I'd phone home to have a more comfortable natter in Welsh, one where I didn't have to think about what I wanted to say before saying it. They also used to joke that they could never understand me at the beginning of any term because my accent had thickened over the holidays. 'Go on, say something in Welsh' became an annoying daily request, as did 'I've never met a real live Welsh person before', a disturbing refrain which led to a conscious decision by me and my new friend from Wales. We saw a poster for the International Ball in the foyer. It was gilt-edged and glamorous. We both looked at each other and smiled.

'No, it's for foreign students,' she said shiftily. We read that everyone was expected to attend in their national dress.

'Well,' I hesitated, looking her in the eye, 'we are in the foreign block.'

'And we certainly sound foreign!' she added.

We got some Welsh costumes sent up from Wales. It would be the first time in my adult life that I'd wear that dress and the first time ever that my friend would. That night we dressed together. We opened a bottle of wine. I helped her with her *brethyn*[4] apron and she helped me with mine. I let my hair down and we put on our Welsh hats. We looked at ourselves in the mirror. Two young Welsh women. My long red hair, her short red hair. Her a non-Welsh speaker from a town in south Wales and me a native speaker from a farm in mid-Wales. Her relationship with Wales was complicated; so was mine. The Geordie taxi driver looked somewhat confused. As we walked into the ballroom, heads turned. We stared back. We stood out a mile but I wasn't sure why. Suddenly, on looking around at the Chinese in their jewelled, coloured silks and the Indians in their shimmering, glittering saris, it struck me. Our national costume was work clothes. The material was thick, scratchy and practical. It was a cheap, hard-wearing cloth. Our shawls were made to carry children and wood for the fire – not to drape decoratively about the shoulders. Our hats were austere, not flamboyant. Our clothes weren't expressive in any way at all. I realised what I had been unconsciously reacting to all these years. I finally felt I had put my finger on it. For me, it didn't express our language, reflect our humour, our laughter and noise. It was deadly silent. We didn't eat a thing that night. We spent the whole time answering questions and being photographed next to short Chinese girls with shining smiles. Feeling slightly uncomfortable, we left and walked to a local nightclub with a

Gallic guy from the Gendarmerie in his navy buttoned uniform, and spent the rest of the night drinking vodka with him and three builders from Middlesborough. I don't think any of us understood a word the others said that night, but we laughed for hours anyway. By the time we arrived back at our digs, dawn was breaking. We sat around the lake in the college grounds, smoking Café Crème cigars, our hats sitting properly and rather starchily by our sides. Neither of us could say very much. My friend was silently regretting that she couldn't speak Welsh. I could think of nothing but my grandmother's work-worn hands.

This 'plainess' and 'modesty' followed me home to Wales. I put such showy expressions of my Welshness away with my quiet Welsh costume. My Welsh hat sat on my wardrobe with quiet dignity and I felt slightly chastised every time I caught sight of it. I started a Masters in writing at Aberystwyth University and resumed the job I had taken in my school holidays at the tourist office. I spent my days studying, selling plasticy Welsh cakes, cheap lovespoons and Valleys humour joke books. We were told that we were the first Welsh people that foreigners would meet on coming to Wales and that we were ambassadors, real Welsh ladies. I couldn't help but smile. This time we were given green and black nylon uniforms that didn't even get wet in the rain and green badges of suitably welcoming roaring dragons. I wrote in English at the time and felt shaky when writing in Welsh. The pendulum has swung the other way by now as this is the first piece of English writing I have produced in four years. It's like exercising muscles. You strengthen one set whilst neglecting another. I remedied the situation by borrowing a first-year Welsh degree reading list from a friend and slowly started to work my way through it. It annoyed and frustrated me in equal measures, but I sat, often at lunchtime at work, between the 'Welcome to Cardiganshire' brochures and the postcards of rosy-cheeked children in traditional Welsh dress, and worked through them. Eventually I quit and moved to north Wales to work at the National Writers' Centre before moving back near home. It was then that I decided to start writing seriously.

There are several of us young Welsh women trying to populate the landscape here in rural Wales, although admittedly I suppose you could call us an endangered species. When there were as few red kites around here as there are of us, they started a breeding programme and saved them (a friend still believes the Welsh Assembly should consider doing the same for us women). The red kites have reached such numbers that they seem to have nothing better to do than wake up less successful species every morning at six o'clock with their self-satisfied mewing. It's true that more change has happened in rural Wales in the last fifty years than in the previous seven hundred. My grandmother's Wales has all but disappeared. Some of the changes are to be welcomed, but all of them have consequences. I know some young women who feel disenfranchised from their identity and find themselves living in quite a schizophrenic state, being at once educated liberated twenty-somethings of the Bellini-drinking variety, and making domestic contributions to farms and homes as such domestic duties are felt by them and those around them to be a highly-prized contribution to the home economy. I feel pride in feeding hungry farmers; after all, I don't get up at five in the morning. Like me, some of my friends have degrees in English but hardly ever use the language. I saw one friend at a village hall gathering the other day. One minute she was slicing bread for the committee tea against her flowery apron listening to an old relative recount a story. When I popped out for some air, she was checking her eBay purchases on her Blackberry outside.

The contemporary Welsh lady also seems to have several jobs, balancing home-keeping with having a full-time job and running a bed and breakfast. Four out of five of my best friends are self-employed for reasons varying from failing to find a satisfying job, failing to find one which actually used their hard-won qualifications or because they had reached the ceiling in their particular careers prematurely – job mobility being virtually non-existent around here. Demographically, young women in rural areas are purchasing more property than ever before. Traditionally, of course, the eldest son inherited farms and properties and the girls used to interchange between the farms through marriage (something which still stands today) but women who have to make it on their own are showing their own initiative now by teaming up with other young women who want to stay here to put a deposit on a rural property. It's virtually impossible for a young woman to manage this on her own due to massively inflated house prices and relatively low incomes.

Personally, I started writing professionally. I live on a farm in the middle of nowhere and write all day. And no, it's not Romantic in any way whatsoever. It rains, the nearest cash-point is twenty-five minutes away by car and any outing with friends has to be planned with military precision. However, I live entirely through the medium of Welsh, I manage to make a living and am certainly very happy. So are all the other young women I know around here. Living here seems to push people's limits and test their resourcefulness.

Caryl Lewis

The Welsh culture, far from being rigid and unwelcoming is limitless in its capaciousness and elasticity. It absorbs, flexes and changes. Women seem to be at the forefront of these changes and they have, in my experience, been misrepresented as jealously guarding and eventually smothering their very delicate culture and language. My *milltir sgwâr*, far from being a landscape of pretty pictures like the postcards in the tourist office, is peopled with faces of friends and relatives past and present, the latter made alive by storytelling. My Welsh women are at once dynamic and traditional; they are both progressive and also rooted in something altogether bigger which sustains them. My difficult relationship with the image of the Welsh woman continues, as it will, I'm sure for a long time to come. Although the traditional image and costume hardly seem to fit the real Welsh women I know, what I learnt through my encounters with the costume is that we need it. Its quiet, dignified, solemn presence serves as an anchor to the past, as a steadying force in the strong current of change in rural Wales. I confess that I too now have a copy of Salem by my desk and although I have put away my costume, I wrapped it lovingly in tissue paper and stored it away with care. My grandmother, her hands smooth from work, left her mark on the landscape and every time I sit down to write I can only hope that she and other Welsh women like her shape the arches of my prints.

Notes

[1] *Milltir sgwâr* – your own back-yard; your 'square mile'.
[2] *Carthen* – a thick woollen blanket made in a traditional way.
[3] *Dau Gi Bach yn Mynd i'r Coed* – a nursery rhyme.
[4] *Brethyn* – a thick woollen traditional cloth used to make clothes.

4

La Vie en Rose

The Art of Celebration

Carol Lee

My friend's habit of smacking buses began one cold January weekend when, coming out of a pub after a long lunch, we found a big coach blocking the last of the daylight.

'Smack it for me,' she ordered suddenly. 'Come on, you do that side and I'll do the other. There.'

The Head of a university department in London by day – and half the night when there are appraisals, assignments and funding applications to do – her job description has been bigger than her for more than a decade. After years of asking to see the powers-that-be about it, the Vice-Chancellor's solution had been simple. She was to work out the bits of her job she couldn't do and, 'Uhum, leave them out.'

'Which bits?' she asked briskly.

Pause. 'That's for you to decide.'

So she is back to smacking buses because it will be all her fault, of course, if she leaves out the wrong bits.

Why she smacks buses – or gets me to do it for her – she thinks is because they are, like the job she once enjoyed, too big, in the way, and spoiling her view. Giving a bus one in the bonnet every now and then is a defiant gesture which shows she is still around and has it in her to make a song and dance, to protest.

I first learned about celebration in the African part of a childhood where we lived in the bush ninety miles outside Bulawayo. There were only two other households. In one a bad-tempered man with a rifle slung permanently under one arm and a crutch to support a wooden leg slung permanently under the other, made me steer clear.

And the other household steered clear of me. Snobbery. My mother, the daughter of a Welsh coalminer, and my father, a lowly English engineer, were not good enough for them even to show their faces.

While I enjoyed the company of animals, making household pets of lizards and chameleons and playing mother to baby dik-dik orphaned by our neighbour's gun, I was deeply lonely. My father was out working all day, and there was no school in which to find friends: instead, I learnt through a correspondence course. Big wedges of work were delivered to a postal address and collected every two weeks while my mother, a potential ally, was too busy defending her kitchen to take much notice of me.

Instead, mosquitoes, ants, beetles, flies of every biting, disease-giving kind vied for her attention. A door open a fraction, a crumb of sugar on the kitchen floor and in they came. A tiny tear in the corner of a piece of protective baize, the whiff of a loaf of bread wrapped in plastic, and all their friends and relations came too.

Stuck between the Invisibles up the path, a gunman below, and little joy at home I took to trailing after our aged gardener, Walter. Exploring at the edge of the hill one day, I saw him in a clearing in his usual squatting position, arms resting on knees, thin stick being twiddled between his fingers.

He was waiting for his cousin, though I did not know this at the time. What I saw was Walter slowly stand up when he heard a lorry stop a long way off on the road below and watch the distant figure of a man jump down from the back of it to begin the walk up towards us. You could tell by his movements and the serious way he held his head and back straight that the man knew he was being watched and waited for. Walter did not wave or move.

When his cousin reached the clearing, Walter still stayed where he was and they stood, for a few minutes, yards away from each other, looking: deep gazes; and eventually the beginnings of slow smiles. They still waited, heads high, perusing each other with their eyes, standing apart, then walking round a bit, circling each other, till at last they were close enough to hug.

Africans waited weeks for people to arrive, years sometimes, as it seemed I did, and I began to learn, like them, not to throw the waiting – and the celebration – away.

My own eyes were a cause of prohibition. 'Don't stare,' I was often instructed. It was no use protesting I was not staring, I was only looking – the largeness of my eyes was the problem, so I learned to shield my gaze. And here were Walter and his cousin, their gazes held, drinking each other in with long deep looks.

An essential part of celebration – holding an occasion and not letting it slip – is in these looks and, in a village one evening in a different part of Africa, I watched them. I was six-teen years old by this time, living in the bush in Tanzania, and three of us white people were invited for a meal: my friend, Linde; her father, John Baker; and me. Being close to the man who would eventually be President, Julius Nyerere, Linde's father was special and I watched him being celebrated, lit up in people's eyes, aflame like the fires which warmed us.

From what I could tell that night, celebrating a person was looking at him as though you were remembering him, like making an indelible picture. Celebration involved capturing the moment, remembrance, a photograph made in the eye and kept in the heart.

Living in Tanzania, in a *large* bush settlement this time, another vivid picture in mind, surreal, like something from Fitzcarraldo. Thousands of square miles of bushland, elephant, rhinoceroses, hyenas and mosquitoes, trillions of these, and in the middle of this, where we stayed, a diamond mine with an old-fashioned clubhouse.

Plateau land, no cities for thousands of miles, the deep blackness of an African night and in the middle of it, this tiny club. Behind it, outside, ringed by fairy lights and coloured red, blue, green and yellow small triangular flags, women in evening dress, men in dinner suits, a dance floor. My first experience of another celebratory art.

Moving with my father's job in a much-travelled childhood, a Christmas spent in Wales gave me a further take on the inner, indelible quality of celebratory remembrance. My mother's parents, my Welsh grandparents, Harry and Bessie's home was our resting place in the UK; I spent time with them and with my cousin, Derek, sitting in the kitchen of their council house in Trimsaran. Carmarthenshire meant long, wet winter nights, which is where, gathered round the Rayburn, Harry came into his own. A wizard with words, he spun Derek and me yarns to make our senses spin.

Our favourite was the one about the night he first met his wife-to-be among the fairlights in the nearby town of Cydweli. As his long-since bride snoozed by the fireplace, hands over stout stomach, toes poking out the end of slippers, Harry drew word pictures of the way our grandmother was at their first meeting. And we could see the dozens of different shades of gold, bronze, saffron, amber in her fiery auburn hair, the fine curve of her ankle bone, dainty feet, proud eyes and tiny, once-upon-a-time waistline. I thought Harry had swallowed a bottle of Evening in Paris the way he told this story. You could smell it. But then, for him it was love, the best kind of celebration.

Celebration has long roots and kindles itself from the fires of memory. Coming from the ability to light up and bring to life inner pictures and narratives, it is of a different order to having a good time, and comes from a different impetus.

After Harry was invalided out of the mines with full-blown pneumoconiosis, my grandparents were poor. Most of the house was like a fridge and there was often no electricity. The pictures Harry combusted into words for us were our store against the cold and dark of that winter and ones in years to follow.

Traditionally, celebration comes from lighting fires to fend off darkness, with bonfire meaning 'good fire' or 'fire of joy'. Its roots stretching back to ancient times, the defiant aspect of celebratory fire was to bring light to darkness. Sunlight meant life and action, darkness brought sleep, that 'little death' and, under cover of it, many dubious and frightening goings-on. Fire banished this foe and was also linked with food. The gathering in of the harvest, a store against the earth's own 'little death', the non-growing time of deep winter, was celebrated with fire, the flame to give light, warmth, and to celebrate the end of work.

It has its roots in darkness, therefore, and in being able to recognise the contrast with light. It contains, at the same time, a need for company, and an end to the hard work of tilling the soil. Winter festivities say, 'We will only work so hard. Now, we will join together and make merry.'

Joining with others against adversity is crucial to the celebratory nature of certain events. When I interviewed British ex-servicemen for a TV programme about their lives as German POWs, they talked to me about the vital role of the camp concert in fending off the hardship of prison conditions and keeping them sane.

Used as an act of communal protest and celebration, hundreds of people had parts and for the weeks leading up to it, the concert was the reason to carry on. It was a way of gathering up pain, indignity, despair and making a bonfire of them. Put on usually at Christmas time, prisoners formed drama groups, comedy acts, duos, trios, bands, orchestras. They made makeshift triangles, drums, zithers and produced sketches, plays, revues.

Lit up on stage on the night, defiance was the leading character; the English language used and spun hard for puns and tricks to heap coals on captors' heads. Carefully crafted word-plays flummoxed interpreters, mocked prison guards and delighted inmates. Loss was present all round – no freedom, no families – but a different sleep after this, a sense of reclaiming something taken away.

Inner retrieval is part of celebrating, and this is a remarkably challenging process at times.

The individual impetus for it goes back to childhood: a wish to recapture lost dreams and freedoms and give a kick in the shins to a status quo which says you are for the world and the world is not for you.

Over-celebratory people, often musicians, artists and the like, are those who get the balance wrong. Bringing too much of their pasts, their childhoods, to the grown-up party called adult life, they wear their hearts on the outside of their jumpers. One such was the late Elizabeth Smart, author of *By Grand Central Station I Sat Down and Wept*. We were buddies in Alberta when a university I was attached to asked her to be Writer-in-Residence, then snubbed her for an excess of writerly habits and celebratory tendencies.

She drank. But then, for her, poetry was personal, and, after a few glasses, she would stop you on your way to the bookshelf. 'No,' she would insist. 'Say it off by heart.' Poetry for Elizabeth was on the inside, not the shelf.

The only time I got drunk with her – never again, the hangover lasted two days – there was deep snow on the ground and we wrapped one extra long scarf round both our necks to keep us from freezing or drifting apart. The pair of us, bound together and staggering, eventually ended up at my front door, me late for the meal the man I lived with had spent the evening preparing.

'Well,' he said, observing the way we hung either side of the doorjamb, scarf taut in between, 'I'm in luck. Not one drunken woman, but two.'

In the bush villages where I grew up there was an African saying that false celebration, or celebrating falsely, brings bad luck. When your heart is insincere, or unready, or when the occasion is not correct for celebration, then you should not do it. For it is wrong to 'put on' a face for celebration when it must be lit from the inside. Your heart has to be in it.

But not to mark a proper occasion at all is also a mistake: *not* to celebrate a birthday, an event, through lack of time or attention. I nearly did it myself one Christmas: lost the plot. Booked to sing a song for a writers' charity cabaret, as the time drew near, I found it clashed with an important meeting. I couldn't do my bit after all. So I rang to tell the concert organiser I had to work. His disappointed tones brought me round. Was I, too, going to be a spoiling, mean, self-denying workaholic, the kind of born-again Puritan who had a briefcase instead of a life? Was I hell! Get out the posh frock, dust down the boa and do the turn, lady. Get on up there and do the turn.

Celebration is not easy to define, but is not to be confused with self-gratification, buffoonery, laddish or ladettish behaviour. You have to be up for it, to have somewhere to come from and go back to. And these are not celebratory times. A commerce-led nightmare has stolen our lights and put them on the outside in shops, stores and cash tills, leaving us dark to ourselves and easily led. Long working hours excuse anything these days. 'I work' is the suggestion, 'therefore I am a good person'.

Essentially, the ability to celebrate depends on whether you think the past is alive or dead, whether the years pile up as tombstones to bury it, or whether personal history, from the first time of remembering, is a living thing to be lit up and called upon. It is *life-ly*, therefore, and, like many family gatherings – especially Christmases – not for the faint-hearted.

I had a bellyful of them myself before a Christmas Eve in Wales when I grasped, at last, the story of my mother's childhood and absconded with her to the beach. We had had a tense relationship over the years – my abandonment to boarding schools and the homes of various relatives unspoken between us. Our bush living providing no schooling, the partings were essential, but what I did not know was how much they pained my mother too. Putting on a brave face, as she thought she should, my mother kept this hurt to herself. As I kept mine.

That night, in the village where I was born and where Harry had spun us his stories, my mother was rummaging round the kitchen. She had forgotten a few things, she said, candles, a few decorations and the like. Did I have time to take her to Llanelli market?

Of course. I had glimpsed something at last, something about the way she felt the need to ask if I had time and thought she might be bothering me.

I had all the time in the world. On occasional weekends in Wales, there was little to do but hope, perhaps, that a way would open in the impasse between us. Leaning against a pillar in the old market hall in Llanelli, with its stalls of cards, fruit and veg, fish, home-made cakes, slippers, underwear, I watched my mother waiting to be served and imagined the place as it was in her childhood, thronging.

I remembered wraiths of stories I had not paid much attention to, about my mother being kept back from school which she loved, to look after her brothers and sisters. Of her having to cook and clean because her own mother hated housework. I thought of my grandparents, Harry and Bessie, bringing their seven children here as I had been told they did, on Christmas Eve, my mother, the eldest daughter, made responsible for watching out for younger siblings. I knew these anecdotes, but not before now, with my mother thinking she might be troubling me, did they come home.

Suddenly, she turned to me, smiled across the crowd, wrinkled her nose. And I saw my mother for the first time as a child standing in the same place, obedient, nervous, alert, expecting to be called away, at any moment, from her pleasure.

When you celebrate, you savour every move of the on-coming person. You do not throw anything away and, as my mother walked back towards me, I saw her with the long gaze of my African and her Welsh past, yards and years of it, her childhood and mine.

'Let's go to the beach.'

Cefn Sidan, only a few minutes away by car, miles of firm golden sand, no buildings in sight, just the sweep of a vast bay, Worm's Head visible on one side, Cydweli on the other, and, in winter, usually not another soul to see them.

We walked till it was nearly dark, wind, waves, sky, not a word spoken – or unspoken – between us.

The chance for closeness, to know and be known, is something you have to be ready for. Sometimes a long time, a winter or half a lifetime. A cause for celebration when it happens, it produces the alive, full-spectrum feel of difference: between light and dark; start and finish; up and down.

In light of this, while the fact that I work, pay my bills, am responsible and useful here and there matters, it is not enough. More important is a rare sighting of an overseas friend on the weekend of his birthday. I spend – fritter? – hours looking in different shops for the exact, right card for him. It is November, drizzling. He hates the rain. The card, 'Singing Butler', by Scottish-born artist Jack Vettriano, has become well known. A couple in evening dress, she barefoot, dancing close together on a beach in a gale. In attendance, maid with apron flying, butler umbrella aloft, clutching something just out of the picture – a bottle of champagne? Inside, a message: 'Let the dance go on, whatever the weather.'

Don't get me wrong: a big smile would have worked just as well, and no time spent. It had to be right, that's all. Which is why celebration is an art. It contains the serious business of our human longing for closeness, connection, continuity and a prospect of vitality to come: a thing of the past brought alive in the present, kept for the future.

At a time when we are encouraged schizophrenically to re-invent ourselves at will, celebration is a force for stability. An adult affair, that says we are human beings with histories, which are what we hold onto in dark times. A form of resistance, celebration has this in common with religion – that it comes from a sense of inner renewal and is the province of the serious, not the sentimentalised, child.

My bus-smacking friend and I are persistent with our celebrations, then. We have a friendship going back fifteen years and her thieving job gets in the way of it. Her birthday; my birthday; her bloke's birthday (only he's not invited); her bloke's mum's passing from this world after years in a coma; me finishing a book; her getting a pay rise, are all up for a song and dance, a protest or two. The death from cancer of a mutual friend at the age of forty-three began our wryly-called 'bonding weekends'. 'Bugger the job, bugger the bloody university,' she said. 'I'm going to enjoy my friends while I can.'

So, three or four times a year we go away together to have time to talk, unwind, be lazy, silly, and show that life outside work can, will – must – be done. The car stacked with Wellingtons, binoculars, anoraks, perfume, pretty blouses, high-heeled shoes, we raid the south coast, Essex or Suffolk for long walks, shoe shops, a celebratory dinner and a place to stay for the night.

Once ensconced, we play ball on the beach, scold seagulls, pick which horse we'd ride on the pier merry-go-round, be flirty with blokes selling the day's fresh catches and tell rambling stories on the sea wall. In between, her phonecall, when it comes, is a reminder of what must be defended in our patch, a call to arms.

'Work's impossible. Are you free on Friday? Good. Meet me in town and we'll molest a 73 on the way home.'

Defiance. Celebration. Dance on, is what I say.

Growing up
with a Fairy Godmother

Rose Wilkins

We are not free to choose by what we shall be enchanted, truly or falsely. In the case of false enchantment all we can do is take immediate flight before the spell really takes hold.

WH Auden

I was about six when I was first told I was descended from a fairy. It was written in the bible – the old Welsh family one, with a host of long-lost great grannies and uncles and cousins recorded on the fly-page. Top of the list was Anne Jones, great granddaughter of one David Jones, an 'honest, skilled and charitable' physician who died in 1719 and whose tombstone stands in the graveyard at Myddfai. According to local lore, the Physicians of Myddfai have been pulling teeth and applying poultices since the thirteenth century, when their founding mother first popped out of a lake.

At the time, I was probably a little disappointed to discover that our family fairy wasn't the sparkly-dressed, silvery-winged variety with a magic wand. Strictly speaking, she's a water nymph – and there's always something a bit fishy about girls with gills. Sirens, mermaids, kelpies... they tend to be rather ambiguous creatures, sexy but slippery. I compromised on imagining her as a Celtic princess, Burne-Jones style, with a sensuous pout and chestnut curls.

The lake known as Llyn y Fan Fach is now a popular walking destination in the Brecon Beacons; a melancholy pool shadowed by dark hills that feature prominently in brochures from the local tourist board. Its story is well known in our part of Wales, and begins when a farmer cutting reeds by the shores of the lake sees a beautiful girl appearing from beneath the water. He woos her with gifts of bread: the first she rejects as too tough, the second as underdone, but the third sample – like Goldilocks' porridge – is 'just right' and she agrees to marry him. As a bonus, she throws in a dowry of magic cattle. However, there's a catch: if her husband should strike her three times, the Lady and her livestock will return to the lake forever.

All goes well until the christening of their first son. The Lady procrastinates, as ladies do, and the husband claps her on the back to ensure she gets a move on. Oops. Turns out she was waiting for the sky to cloud over because of a premonition that their baby would die if she took him out in the sun that day.

More children are born, all goes well, and the happy couple set off to a cousin's wedding. During the ceremony the Lady begins to wail and her husband taps her reprovingly. He's not to know she has foreseen the death of the bride and her unborn child. Two strikes down, one to go....

In the fullness of time, the tragic deaths foretold by the Lady come to pass. She and her family are attending the funeral when the Lady begins to laugh in delight – for she can see the dead girl being joyfully received into heaven. Her husband, unfortunately, is so mortified by her inappropriate behaviour that he slaps her to bring her to her senses. The next moment his wife is hot-footing it back to the lake, taking her magical livestock with her. She returns only once, appearing by the shores of Llyn y Fan Fach to teach her three sons her healing arts, and to show them where to gather medicinal herbs.

A happy ending of sorts I suppose, though I remember my sympathies were sadly torn between the absconding nymph and her abandoned family. 'But he didn't *really* hit her – not properly,' I complained. 'She should have realised it was a mistake.' My father tried to explain that just as the farmer couldn't understand his wife's otherworldly gifts, she wouldn't ever understand the rough and tumble of human interaction. This I could accept. After all, I knew grown-ups acted according to a mysterious logic all of their own, and yet there were times when my own perfectly sensible reasoning appeared to baffle and exasperate them in equal measure. Sometimes life was like that.

Sad to say, I spent a certain amount of my childhood and early adolescence fantasising about the day when my fairy godmamma would make her long-overdue reappearance. By the age of thirteen, I had it all planned out. I would have my heart broken by some delectably wicked seducer (Mr Darcy with a dash of Jagger), whereupon I would flee to my ancestral heartlands and, in a gathering storm, pace the shores of the lake. Naturally, I would have a new outfit for the occasion: something silk and slinky, perhaps, to complement the pre-Raphaelite curls I was also set on acquiring. A bit of hand-wringing later and – hey presto! – a glorious maiden would emerge (Lady Di with a hint of Bette Davis). 'Fear not, my child,' she would say, 'for I am the Lady of the Lake and....'

But that's where things got a bit fuzzy. I didn't think I was particularly suited to a career in medicine (too many bodily fluids) and herb gathering didn't sound much fun either (too much mud and nettles). A quick dip into the *Meddygon Myddfai* shows that the Physicians took an, er, inventive attitude to natural remedies. Had the Lady herself tried out a poultice of peacock droppings as a cure for haemorrhoids, or did this pass for water nymph humour? Either way, I was hoping for the granting of wishes and righting of wrongs, not the thirteenth-century equivalent of an aspirin and a First Aid manual.

About once a year, usually around Easter, the family would go on a picnic excursion to Llyn y Fan Fach. Visits always began with a trip to Myddfai's churchyard, paying homage at the tombstone of Grandpa Jones, with an assortment of politely baffled houseguests in tow. The party would then trek up the Designated Footpath to eat cheese sandwiches in the drizzle and watch hyper kids in day-glo anoraks chuck crisps into the lake. The closest we ever got to the world of legend was when my sister found a cow's jawbone in the mud. We decided it must be the noble remains of the fairy cattle, some of which evidently hadn't made it back into the lake on time. Still, I wasn't wholly disheartened. A water nymph, I reasoned, needn't be confined to her lake of origin. She might appear from anywhere aquatic – in a canal or bathtub, out of a hosepipe....

Of course I didn't *really* believe I had a fairy godmother.

Well, not entirely. But the story was only the start of a reading binge on all things legendary. I went from the Lady of the Lake to the Mabinogion, the Arabian Nights, Norse sagas, Homeric epics, Arthurian romance. I returned again and again to the old favourites like Perrault, Hans Andersen and the Brothers Grimm. Unfortunately, some might argue that this is not a reading habit either grown women or small girls should aspire to. Indeed, just before I began to write this piece, research by Susan Darker-Smith, a graduate student in behavioural psychotherapy, was widely reported in the press as claiming that early exposure to fairy tales subliminally encourages girls to grow up into victims of domestic violence. Old favourites such as *Cinderella* and *Beauty and the Beast* apparently provide 'templates' of dominated women. Fairy Tales End In Horror! Cinderella Linked To Violent Relationships! the column inches squealed.

Which is a theory that demonstrates as much common sense as a poultice of peacock dung, frankly. Reading is never a passive experience, not even for a naturally timid child, and to claim that a girl who loves Rapunzel will grow up to become a victim of abuse is like arguing that someone who passionately admires *Lolita* is bound to start lusting after twelve-year-olds. The world of legend may deal with stereotypes – or archetypes, if you prefer – but within its range of peasant girls, princesses and goddesses there is plenty of pluck and heroism to be found, as well as sweetness and submission.

The joy of fairy stories is that their multiplicity means they can be pretty much anything you want them to be; *Cinderella* alone is said to boast 345 variations. Freud turned them into icky Oedipal nightmares (the *Tale of Red Riding Hood* as a parable of penis envy, anyone?). Disney fashioned them into saccharine homilies on 1950s domestic values. The likes of Angela Carter, Marina Warner and AS Byatt have subverted them for the sisterhood. Over the years, I've been fascinated by the wealth of literary and psychoanalytic criticism on the subject, but these tales ultimately deny conclusive analysis.

So where does this leave my Lady? You might conclude that she was a heartless floozy who abandoned husband and kids at the first sign of trouble. That her horny-handed peasant was only ever going to be a sideline. Others might say that the first time the farmer whacked her one she should have been out of that door and into the lake before you could say 'restraining order'. It's true that fairy girls and mortal men have a long history of mutual incompatibility, all too frequently ending in tears. It is perhaps the ultimate upstairs/downstairs, love-across-the-divide. One knows right from the start that the farmer's going to blow his three chances. Us mortals always do.

However, most of the fairy women of legend are cold-hearted sirens such as *La Belle Dame Sans Merci*, so it's nice to hear of a nymph who chooses human warmth above a magic kingdom. The Lady is imperious, implacable even, but you don't get the impression she's a wanton heartbreaker. After all, this is a woman who judged her suitor on his bread-baking technique and is practical enough to bring a herd of prize cattle for a dowry. She may have had to forsake her children but at least she made sure they were set up in a respectable career, with good prospects. (A few years down the line and Rhiwallon & Sons were court doctors to the local bigwig, Rhys Gryg, and building up a nice little nest-egg in land and honours.) As for her pre-nuptial agreement, I particularly like the detail that when she returns to the lake she takes her

166

super-league cows with her. Bet she got the best set of china and the prize love-spoons, too.

All things considered, I don't think I've developed a predilection for abusive relationships from my ancestress' example, though I can't help wondering how the story would have turned out if the Lady had had three daughters, instead of sons. Would her parting gift have been different? A love-potion rather than a recipe for cough syrup, a dowry rather than a career? It's a fact that there has always been a high proportion of medics in my family, but history doesn't relate if any of the Physicians of Myddfai were female. My grandmother, Mary Powell, had ambitions to train as a doctor, but as a genteel young lady in the Thirties she had to settle for being a medical secretary instead. There's scant controversy in saying things are different now – as not particularly genteel schoolgirls in the Nineties, my classmates and I were of the opinion that we could become doctors or firemen or High Druid Priestesses if we wanted to be.

But what if, during those gloomy adolescent years, a magic godmother really had popped out of the waterworks? Let's say she really did offer me my heart's desire. What would I have wished for? Beauty. Prince Charming. An Ivory Tower. Probably in that order. My upbringing and education was at pains to teach me that success is not kissing a handsome prince, virtue is not a pretty face, and happiness is not a combination of the two. Aged thirteen, I didn't believe it. Aged twenty-six I do – about 75% of the time. That other 25% is distracted by the aspirational neuroses celebrated by popular culture, and fed by the obsessive intimacies of the changing room, the Problem Page and the Girl's Night Out. My generation is still preoccupied by wishes we are half-ashamed to admit to, so perhaps it's just as well fairy god-mothers are thin on the ground.

Whatever one's path in life may be, however, my learned ancestors are full of tips for leading a healthy and happy one. Unchaste desires? Eat rue in the morning. Excessive intoxication? Down an egg-shell full of hemp agrimony. Vomiting as a result of said intoxication? Try washing your genitals in vinegar. They even have an all-purpose remedy for beating the blues: *If you would be at all times merry, eat saffron in meat or drink, and you will never be sad: but beware of eating over much, lest you should die of excessive joy.* Bet it must have been wild down medieval Myddfai on a Friday night.

Not that I've ever read the *Meddygon* in the language it was originally written, for our Welsh family bible, with its Hopkins and Davises and Powells, is out of date. As the eighteenth century slid into the nineteenth, family fortunes went up in the world. The Powells became gentrified and started pronouncing themselves the more Anglo-friendly Poles. They sent their sons to English public schools, went on campaign in the Raj, prayed at church, not chapel, and forgot their Welsh.

My mother is American, I grew up between Carmarthenshire and London, went to boarding school in Cardiff followed by university in England. Now I'm a Londoner, first and foremost, which is a breed apart. But if I tell people I'm half Welsh they say 'But you don't sound it!' and occasionally, mystifyingly, 'You don't look it!' People like the Celtic thing but generally speaking, the Welsh still aren't as sexy as the Irish or the Scots.

Still, when I say 'home' I mean home in Wales, a small,

rather shabby country house in Carmarthenshire, under the shadow of Carreg Cennen Castle. It is almost ridiculously romantic: an orchard of ancient apple trees and tumbledown walls, a ruined castle across the way where ravens nest, ancient mountains dotted with wild ponies and the ruins of iron-age forts. Family outings to Llyn-y-fan Fach may have been disappointingly short on nymphs, but a little mental embroidery can take you a long way. Squint, and those castle walls could be the ruins of Valhalla or Camelot, the sun flashing off the armour of knights, not plastic-wrapped silage bales. Friends who come to visit think it's all Terribly Tolkien, Peter Jackson-style. 'Looks a bit like New Zealand, but smaller,' they say, surveying the valley.

I've never been to New Zealand but I think I know what they mean. Wales does Epic and Romantic alright, but on a small scale. Cosy, and a little cluttered. And for me, it's not quite real, either, perhaps because home is a place I'm always preparing to leave. When I was little, Wales was where we spent our holidays; once the family moved there permanently I was off to boarding school, then university, then work in London. So I know I'm guilty of what a lot of well-meaning incomers with holiday cottages tend to do – of romancing, prettifying the place to fit. The rose-tinted Cymru of my heart doesn't have much room for Charlotte Church or Rhodri Morgan or blood, sweat and scrums at the Millennium Stadium. Even now, although I love having friends down for the weekend to 'show them the sights', part of me slightly resents the intrusion. I have been homesick for Wales my whole life but I have never lived there for more than a month or so at a time.

The trouble was, my childhood in the Cennen Valley was

picturesque and old-fashioned in equal measure. Even at the time it didn't seem to bear much relation to life in the wider world. My sister and I had few local friends of our own age and were thrown pretty much exclusively on each other's company. Together, we roamed the countryside, building huts in the woods and dams in the streams. The garden was our private kingdom, where we could play at castles in the trees and jungles in the shrubbery. The old house, with its cabinets of curios, and long-dead relations smiling from the walls, was great for hide-and-seek, even better for treasure seeking. (As I write this I am horribly aware of sounding like Enid Blyton meets a Werther's Original ad. But it's all true.)

Going away to boarding school was a shock, the world of my classmates even more so. These up-to-the-minute girls with their chatter about boys and rock concerts and make-up seemed an alien breed. I lived in a country house and sounded 'English Posh' but my parents were permanently strapped for cash – my mum cut my hair, I was in NHS specs and dressed in hand-me-downs. Dark rumours circulated that my father, an artist, painted naked ladies for a living. I was hideously lonely and resentful and refused to contemplate being happy anywhere but home.

Returning there every Friday felt like Christmas and my birthday and the first day of the holidays wrapped into one; every Sunday felt like the beginning of a life-sentence. I knew I was the subject of many anxious late night discussions between my parents, but although they gave me the option of changing schools, I was determined to stick it out. Sheer bloody-mindedness, I suppose, in combination with a sneaking suspicion that I would be equally miserable elsewhere. In hindsight, I took a perverse pride in not fitting in (or *giving* in, to my muddled kind of thinking). Loneliness had made me arrogant.

Loneliness also sealed my daydream habit – I've mentioned the Escape to Llyn y Fan Fach fantasy, but there were plenty of others. The ugly duckling who would – surely – turn into a swan. The exiled princess, caught between two worlds. I am glad to say that my grown-up life in London is a busy and pleasant one, and I have stopped pining for lost kingdoms that never were. But going 'home', going 'back', is still a retreat into childhood and the landscape of legend. Real life becomes curiously suspended, part of me half-expects to emerge, Rip Van Winkle-like, from my weekend away only to find the outer world altered beyond compare. I know I am not the only person to construct my 'internal autobiography' in this way; it is an all-too-common temptation to try and frame one's personal experiences in literary terms, to order the randomness of life into a narrative framework from a favourite book, whether that's an Austen romance or a Tolkien epic. The stories we choose to lose ourselves in both sustain and distort our vision of the world.

I may have come to terms with the fact that life is never going to be a fairy tale but I have done my level best to make a living out of them. My day job is at a children's publisher, though the Hans Andersen tradition faces fierce competition with stories about exploding toilets or teenage crack-addicts or faery punks waging guerrilla warfare. In fact, if you're looking for sweet old-fashioned tales like your granny told you, your best bet is to head for the sparkly pink beach book all about snogging 'n' shopping. I never planned to become a writer of chick-lit, but as career paths go, it makes a kind of sense. After all, this is a genre that's all about wish fulfilment and happy endings and other unlikely things. It provides the comforts of childhood dreaming: of magical transformations, of knights-in-shining-armour (often disguised), of witchy bitch-queens and plucky heroines struggling to make sense of it all.

Sometimes this makes me uneasy. My writing is a source of pride, pleasure and a comfortable income, but people find it difficult to understand that, at the end of the day, it's just my job, not a 'vocation'. And, like any job, it has responsibilities that go beyond the ones outlined in the contract. I know that reading is not a passive experience, but I also know the stories you choose to escape into have a different power than the ones you read for information or instruction. Fairy stories can be whatever you want them to be but, let's face it, my particular brand of fiction is generally perceived as having as much depth as a coat of nail polish. All too often in this kind of book, you scratch the surface girl-power gloss and find a moral as old-fashioned and inflexible as a whale-bone corset: happiness is kissing a prince, success is transforming from the duckling to the swan. It is fairy-tale lite, with happily-ever-after guaranteed, and nothing darkly unpredictable or bloodthirsty or bizarre to spoil that fantasy glow.

I try to compromise. In my first book, my teenage heroine dumped Mr Fabulous and waltzed off into the sunset as a merry singleton – to the slight disconcertion of my American publisher. At the moment I'm working on the story of, yes, an ugly duckling who finds a magic ring. There's a handsome young genie inside, ready to grant her every desire. She won't be crowned prom-queen at the end of the tale, but she won't end up pregnant and broke on a council estate either. This time, my gal gets her prince.

The truth of the matter is, happy endings are even more

fun to write than to read. The Physicians warn of the dire consequences of 'excessive joy' but I like to think I'm doing the literary equivalent of sprinkling a little saffron in the soup. Or pulling a big fat chocolate cake from out of the oven and giving a slice to thousands of people I've never met. Sometimes, however, this kind of conclusion can feel like cheating, although who you're cheating – or how – isn't entirely clear. I am still wary of nurturing false comfort, of promoting wishes that are better left unfulfilled, enchantments that deceive as well as delight. You can be a feminist who loves fairy stories, but can you be a feminist who writes chick-lit? I wish I could decide.

But then, 'be careful what you wish for' is the moral of the simplest stories, and some of the greatest literature too. It applies to the humble farmer desiring a creature not of this world, or a fairy nymph wishing to feel human warmth. Or a schoolgirl, hoping for romance and rescue and pre-Raphaelite curls.

Somewhere, I hope, my fairy grandmamma is laughing.

Prosperina's Last Gasp

Charmian Savill

Be not afeard: the isle is full of noises,
Sounds and sweet airs, that give delight, and hurt not.

The Tempest (1611) Act 3, Scene 2

The more I cook for people the more I realise that I am creating plays, dramas full of the most interesting characters I know. As a theatre director I am always casting my net for the best catch: I seek beauty, expressiveness and precision. As a cook, many of my directing skills are apparent, but it is whether my food sings or not that is the real test.

On my 'little sceptred isle' there have been lost kings, queens and courtiers; Miranda, Ferdinand, Caliban, and myself, a dissolute Prosperina clutching her 'books' to her bosom, weighed down with her good intentions, distracted by her desires, set on not only feeding but staging a culinary occasion.

175

And not forgetting Ariel, my other more obliging self, who serves me and others when I am distracted or despondent. No constant self exists.

Prosperina is, very often, a cantankerous old she-wizard once the day dawns; she hasn't had enough sleep and drank five too many glasses of wine. At seven she gets up, groaning, wishing everything would just go away. But Ariel, frail and willing creature, washes up, makes tea, feeds the birds, empties the dishwasher, cleans the downstairs loo, finds napkins, picks flowers, marinates the meat, makes a quick raspberry crumble and has toast ready for Prosperina by nine, which is when children and husband appear. Ariel cheerfully (a spirit and inhuman therefore) asks everybody how they are and makes tea and watches their toast for them.

Prosperina inwardly seethes at their brightness and gives them all tasks: dusting, shopping (she makes a list while eating her toast), peeling vegetables, laying tables. They all announce their own highest priorities which put these given tasks in the lowest category, and a bad-tempered Prosperina, still in her sky-blue gown, shuffles into action by checking her menu for the day. This cheers her up as she has made two of the things on the list already. There are eleven other things to do, but deep down she is an optimist.

It is a lunch today and there are two and a half hours to go before the first of the guests arrive. I feel a witchiness coming upon me, and the (c)oven calls. The world of Wicca, with its dictate 'harm none', has become a familiar reference point in our house: teenage women, including my daughter, seem to prefer its structures to those of the Church in Wales; its powerful identification with, and worship of nature is understandable.

My daughter has made tomato bread which we will warm in the oven to eat with the fish soup, our beginning. Finding succulent mouthfuls of fish in a fennel and tomato-flavoured fish stock spiced with chilli and gently toasted garlic cheers people. Ariel amalgamates the ingredients, leaving the inclusion of the fish until just before the soup is served, so that it slips onto the tongue.

Prosperina gets in the way, worrying about her own presentation; how much make-up for the middle of the day? What allows for maximum expansion of the waist without looking like something comfortable – how attractive do I need to be? I do not feel attractive, my skin is dry and my head and stomach feel tetchy. I make a strong coffee.

The food will be my front, no one will see me; I'll be so busy, serving and dishing up, close observation of my weary self will be difficult; so I must keep moving, and be Ariel, self-effacing invisible spirit. The coffee is working, Ariel is busying herself. A banquet will appear.

My marinating lamb loins glisten with olive oil, lemon zest and fresh rosemary perfuming the air around them. Ariel prepares a tray of field mushrooms, stuffing them with garlic, chopped olives and fresh parsley, oregano and rosemary. In passing, Prosperina steals her hand up her husband's galley T-shirt and caresses his nipples, which she knows he finds pleasurably teasing; she checks the response and extent of his purple wand, then shoots off to put out clean hand towels. Lacking the benefit of a kitchen alter ego, he returns more vigorously to peeling vegetables, checking the wine he has chosen is in the right place (chilling or warming), and dithering over the selection of music. Prosperina returns, towels distributed, *maquillage appliqué*, cleavage dramatised. She dispatches him above deck, identifying the appropriate colour of formal shirt he is to don for the banquet.

The occasion is a writers' lunch, held in honour of a young Russian girl who is staying with us. Obsessed with Oscar Wilde, she dresses in a long black skirt, antique white blouse, tight belt and a black tie; she reminds me of what I imagine a young intellectual looked like in the early 1900s. Her ambition is to be a novelist, like her father; she writes frenetically, walking herself around a room faster and faster into a moment where she can transfer her movement into writing. It reminds me of a person trying to get breath during an asthmatic attack. While laying the table, Anya shyly asks whether she looks alright. I reassure her. Anya intuits the necessary theatre of lunch, where everyone will play a part. She will sometimes be a spirit figure in the masque; the young remind and teach us to respect the power of living and feeling in the moment.

The table is laid, two tables actually, very old wobbly gate-legs shoved together disguised with a large white tasselled bedspread, white linen napkins, small bowls of garden roses and cutlery purchased with petrol tokens in the early 1980s.

The dining room adjoins the kitchen, all new and recently constructed, though none of it has been painted and the windows still have packaging tape all over their frames. There are French windows that lead out from the dining area onto a slated flat area with an un-mown area of weeds, brambles, bugle, dock, buttercup and dandelion beyond. I like the colour of plaster unpainted, and always tell people it's the colour they paint prison cells to keep the inmates calm.

Three men, well-known writers, are due to join us; and two women, a jazz composer and a medical statistician. Prosperina says to her husband, 'There will be a storm this afternoon,' he anxiously raises his head, causing Ariel to crackle into action, 'but it will be good.'

He deliberately asks questions that provoke deep responses from those around the table. Ariel sweeps away to check the last minute details of the menu, quickly rustles up two large bowls of olives, one with garlic and basil and the other with lemon zest and chopped rosemary, and Prosperina cannot imagine how she will ever do without her Ariel.

Prosperina begins to unravel her island experience, further revealing her bosom, her lips shining, and her face beginning to rise to the occasion, because it must. The first few sips of wine make her benign again and the young Russian almost clicks her heels together and dips her head in respect as she is introduced to the three writers. The Jewish writer watches carefully, the Welsh writer's excess physical energy and shyness get in the way of contact for the first fifteen minutes and the Irish writer, who has teenage children of his own, smiles and senses the situation.

After soup and appreciative noises, I start grilling lamb loins. This takes too long. Ariel clears the table, fills wine glasses, and tries to make the loin situation part of the play. I look at the table: everyone is talking, Anya is deeply engaged in a discussion with the Jewish writer, and my loins begin to colour under the grill. The wine begins to take effect and there are louder voices and wilder gestures. I sense thunder clouds: Israel, Bush and Blair. The lamb is succulent, except for my husband's and Anya's, as I see them struggle crossly with unexpected sinews. I am mortified. The wine flows and people start to take sides.

Pudding. A rich chocolate Spanish torte with orange ice-cream, surrounded by a smooth alcoholic orange custard.

Sweetens the dynamic, and then it erupts. Four-letter expletives land all over the table like discarded shuttlecocks.

It is five o'clock, and a hot and sunny day. People move outside who judge themselves to be no part of the argument. Anya, who is fifteen, shares her poetry with the Irish writer. My children, a girl of fourteen and an eleven-year-old boy, listen and share talk with the composer at the same time. My daughter is outraged by a comment by the medical statistician, who announces that we should not take Anya's ambitions as a writer seriously. I am outraged too, having struggled as a child to be taken seriously, and failed, losing all my own stories during the frequent moves to solve the debts my father constantly struggled with. But she is a medical statistician and has to be right. Ariel flies in and excuses the comment, placing the fault at alcohol's door. The Irish writer remembers his younger self and how long it took him to become successful. Inside, the storm abates; the Jewish writer speaks of the difficulty of early success followed by years of invisibility, the Welsh writer talks of his recent work on a libretto, the composer describes the jazz suites she has written on themes of Celtic mythology and the perils of beauty. I marvel at the spells they invent.

The drunken statistician disrupts the easy exchanges at the table with accusations that my husband is in thrall to the Jewish writer. The statement feels like some deep fury she has formulated before this occasion. My husband responds, saying he has only respect for the writer. I laugh to myself bitterly, but am falling into the ditch of despair, and call Ariel for assistance: she needs to employ her lightness of touch, that sweet song of hers. Ariel presents a selection of cheeses, Welsh and English; bowls of cherries, radishes and grapes work like flowers, encouraging hope and appetite. I marvel at the relentless procession of food and suppress the anxiety about the cost of it all. My gamble with the theatre of the table provokes a crisis in Prosperina: I wonder why I do it, constantly; it begins to keep me awake at night.

The next day is a bright summer morning, a rare moment in Wales, and the time has come to question the power of the books and the conjuring up of blissful exchanges of talk and food. Prosperina contemplates the attendant fear she has of laying aside her books and magic and getting off the island. She wonders about the meaning of making banquets; where do they take her?

The books lure her most mornings, the spells accompany her at breakfast; the deep pull of their magic never ceases to arouse. Without these what would happen to her self? What would happen to her relationship with all the different artists who gather in her home? Prosperina begins to faintly understand what she is, and it is difficult.

> *Our revels now are ended. These our actors,*
> *As I foretold you, were all spirits and*
> *Are melted into air, into thin air:*
> *And, like the baseless fabric of this vision,*
> *The cloud-capped towers, the gorgeous palaces,*
> *The solemn temples, the great globe itself,*
> *Yea, all which it inherit, shall dissolve*
> *And, like this insubstantial pageant faded,*
> *Leave not a rack behind.*
>
> The Tempest, Act 4, Scene 1

She conjures up banquets as a way of substituting for loss. She is afraid of unstructured time. None of the artists do what she does, which makes her unique at least, but it's a vital revelation. Is it power Prosperina wants, or the perfection of her art? If the ship has come to collect her and the courtiers are on her side, how will she live away from her island? Without Ariel and all the spirit world gathering and coping for her in moments of culinary crisis, will she be lonely?

5

Don't Explain

Loved to Distraction

Mavis Nicholson

In 1987, Valerie Grove published a book called *The Compleat Woman: Marriage, Motherhood, Career: Can she have it all?* I was among those included in the anthology, along with Alice Thomas Ellis, Mary Warnock, Margaret Forster, Sheila Kitzinger and others. Our common bond was that, like Valerie Grove, we had to have been married for twenty-five years to the same man. We had to be mothers with at least three children – and we had to have careers. In other words, we had to 'have it all'.

Well, six years ago, when I was sixty-eight, I ceased to be A *Compleat Woman,* as Geoff, my husband of nearly fifty years, died. I can't begin to talk about my old age without talking about this major amputation.

It hurled my life right up to the edge of a cliff from which I am slowly, painfully dragging myself away... sort of. I am not intending to wallow in self-pity, but, as a woman in her mid-seventies, the death of my husband has been the most difficult event of my life, and has, in many ways, changed the way I live.

All my life I have been first in somebody's life. First of all, in my parents' lives. We were a hard-up, working class family where children came not only first but second and third. I was the first child and I was over five before my brother and sister were born (they were twins). My mother told me once that I was never out of somebody's arms. The moment I started to grizzle, let alone cry, I was wrapped in a shawl and nursed to sleep. 'Loved to distraction, you were,' said my mother. Which is the only thing I have ever wanted to be. I'm not ambitious for admiration, only for love. Later, I found it, oddly, on the telly. My work might have been admired but the viewers often wrote in about how they loved my programme. And when they recognised me on the street, they'd come up warmly and greet me like affectionate friends.

And then came Geoff, whom I met at university. It was quite romantic. He was a year older, having done his National Service. I was going to the Birmingham Arts Festival, to play Mrs Dudgeon in *The Devil's Disciple*. He was going as a reporter for the college paper. He was Norma's boyfriend at the time, part of our gang of eight young women whose rooms were on the same landing in the college hostel. Before we left, Norma, said, 'Do look after Geoff for me when you get there.' It was New Year's Eve and we'd all gone to various parties, and as the clock struck twelve, Geoff walked towards me, very poetic-looking, very thin, long hair which no one had then, and red shirt which no one wore, and said 'Happy New Year' and kissed me. Something amazing happened as we kissed that made it impossible for us ever to be separate again, despite the initial difficulties of both of our relationships with Norma. I was a very big first in his life as he was in my life for the rest of our long (how I wish it could have been longer) time together.

And then, when I became a mother, I was first in the lives of my three sons. I was happy being Mrs Woodentop at home with my babes while Mr Woodentop brought home the money. At this time, I had long black hair down to my backside, and fantasised on the way to the park, pushing the youngest in the pram with the other two kids holding onto the handles, that I'd be discovered by a film director. Bringing up children you dabble in being a 'Jill' of all trades – a bit of a teacher, nurse, doctor, taxi-driver, head cook.... I look back on those days as the darling buds of May days, and I am glad I didn't go out to work and miss them.

Despite my fantasies about being 'discovered', I didn't feel isolated as a mother who stayed at home and didn't work. Nor anxious to go out into the world and start carving a career for myself. It was quite the norm for the woman not to work while the kids were babies and toddlers in those days. So there were many chums like me pushing their prams around the park.

I married at twenty-one and didn't have the first baby until I was twenty-seven. Which meant that I had a little peep at work, enough to realise that I didn't want to go into an office every day, so that was out as a career. I had worked in what was regarded as a glamorous job: a copy-writer in advertising. But as a strong Welsh Labour girl I didn't really approve of advertising so it was a stopgap as far as I was concerned and it was no hardship to give it up for the really important job of rearing children. And because I'd had my look around before the children arrived, I didn't feel I was missing too much. When and where I grew up, in Briton Ferry, near Swansea, mothers lost their figures early and gave up a lot of their lives to their children, and looked as if they weren't going to do anything again, ever.

Even though it was my choice to be full-time mum (or rather I never questioned the role at that time) I used to get annoyed with Geoff because he could go off to work and be free as a bird as I saw it, while I was stuck at home. He pointed out to me that he was free all right if you liked going to rugby matches in the rain and freezing cold as he did when he was sportswriter on the *Observer*. But you go away to France for a month on the Tour de France, I'd snipe. Since when have you ever watched a bike race, he'd ask me.

It was Geoff, though, who kept me aware of life outside the home when I was in danger of becoming too immersed in babies. He drew my attention to things that were happening with women's lib – it was only later that I became actively involved myself, both professionally, as Home Editor of *Nova* magazine, and through resistance to, for instance, threats against a woman's right to choose. My experience of domestic bliss as a mother and housewife in no way conflicted with my belief that the 1967 Abortion Act should not be amended, in 1980, to make abortion more difficult for women.

Geoff also fully encouraged me to take my chance when offered it and go to work in telly. My first job meant recording the *Good Afternoon* programme in the morning and I would be back for lunch which Geoff had cooked ready for me. And then I was outside school at four o'clock, meeting the three boys. He was amazingly unjealous of any success I had and if I earned more money that didn't bother him. We always shared everything.

My mother, I now remember, had previously tried to curb my occasional impatience about not working by saying that your children's childhood is fleeting and not to be missed and you could have plenty of time after they are at school to find a job.

I do not regret listening to that advice, for somehow I relived my own childhood through experiencing those early years of my three boys. It helped me when I came to write the autobiography of my girlhood, *Martha Jane and Me*. I loved seeing the world through my sons' eyes and being the full-time centre of my toddlers' comical lives.

And now I am not first in anyone's life. And, whew, even just writing that is nearly enough to knock the stuffing out of me. I say nearly, because Geoff somehow went some way in preparing me for this gigantic ordeal. He helped make it possible for me to survive, as I hope I helped him die with some positive thoughts.

Once he knew his colon cancer had spread and he would die within the year, he refused further chemotherapy. The surgeon was frank with him and said it might prolong Geoff's life a little but it certainly would destroy the quality of life he was experiencing at this time.

Geoff asked me if I agreed with his choice to discontinue the chemo before he finally made it. I did. And then, when we were on our own, he told me that most of all he wanted to die at home, and would that be possible from my point of view? It certainly was. And it was our steadfast aim through all the time he was terminally ill. We made it by the skin of our teeth.

It was a beautiful year. We had both been open with all our relatives and friends and acquaintances about how serious Geoff's illness was. They wanted to spend time with us. We tried to make the most out of it but softly and gently and as naturally as we could. We didn't dash to fly on Concorde. Nor take off for Bermuda. Geoff was keen to stay home and put a few things in order so that I could take over the bills and the money side that I had never bothered my pretty little head with before. You simply can't try to wring every ounce of pleasure out of every single minute of each day even though they were speedily winkling down to a precious few.

So, life carried on while Geoff felt reasonably well. On his seventieth birthday all our family met in Disneyland outside Paris: three sons and their wives and our three grandchildren with one grandson, Owen Geoffrey to be, incubating inside Martha. He was born four days before Geoff died, as it turned out.

We chose Disneyland, though it was not quite us really, because we hoped it would keep the grandchildren amused so that we could be near Paris on Geoff's actual birthday. We had booked a fine lunch in a traditional classy French restaurant with all the paraphernalia of huge dazzling crisp white table-cloths and napkins and waiters in voluminous aprons and a profuse catch of shellfish displayed on a gigantic multi-layered glass stand full of ice blocks, served with wonderfully ornate silver tongs.

We were in no rush to do things that weren't natural to our lives except for that one outing, which Geoff's failing energy could just about manage. After this he started to feel ill and couldn't eat much. So then I ate simply, like him. The smell of food nauseated him. So I avoided cooking. 'It must be a bit like being really old,' he told me once, 'this dying. You aren't able to be so interested in life because you simply haven't the emotional and physical energy to respond.'

190

Because at mealtimes we weren't eating and drinking wine, which we had always loved doing, I used to put on music while Geoff sipped his multivitamin drinks. But one night he said, 'Sweetheart, this is a terrible thing to say, but music demands too much from me. I just find it too painful to respond to its feelings.'

And another time he warned me that he couldn't any longer put his arm round me as we lay side by side in bed as he had no strength. I put mine lightly round him until he couldn't stand that either. This too must happen to people as you both get more ancient and doddery, weaker and arthritic.

It was almost Geoff's last time out in the garden, and Harry, our youngest son, pointed to a baby greater spotted woodpecker in our garden. Adult woodpeckers had been coming every year for years to pick the seeds off the red-hot pokers, but this baby was a new event. There's nothing to beat a first time/last time moment.

On the very last time, sitting on a bench facing the distant hills beyond the fields and the river, which is our view from our house in mid-Wales, Geoff wanted me to know that he could not have been happy with anyone else; and although he did not want to die he felt pleased that he had achieved more than he had ever expected to.

Yet it seemed preposterous he was going to die. This healthy-bodied, strong-minded man. Strong except for the murderous cancer that was a parasite feeding off him that would kill him and then die itself. What a waste. 'I worry how you will be, though, on your own,' said Geoff, 'facing the rest of your life and old age on your own. There's one thing I have a strong view about: stay, whatever you do, stay independent of the family.'

191

'How do you think you'd have managed if I were the one dying?' I asked Geoff. He'd have caught the bus like Robert John (a one-time neighbour of ours) into Oswestry once a week and brought back what he could have carried. Lived a bit like a hermit, he thought.

I haven't lived like a hermit but I have survived, to my utter amazement, in a remote house by myself. I try to work out how a gregarious person like I am could do this. A lot of people have asked, 'Aren't you scared?' But I'm not scared. When Geoff died, the worst thing that could happen to me had happened and I guess I wasn't scared of anything after that. I don't like it but I know, to some extent, I am coping with being on my own at seventy-four years of age.

I have wondered how he and I would have coped with 'it' together – real old age. We might have dragged each other down. Now we'll avoid all that, I remember thinking – clinging to some tiny bit of salvage when he and I were drowning.

It is difficult to be honest about death and it is still the case that most old people pussy-foot about death and dying. The doctor and our health carers, who started popping in as things got worse, were delighted and quite moved by our openness about Geoff's fatal illness. It was a great relief to them. They often had to be diplomatic if, say, the husband didn't want his wife to know how bad he was, or vice versa.

Perhaps ironically, I would never have been able to handle it if it hadn't been for Geoff. Death scared the living daylights out of me. I still feel ghastly about mine. More how I'll die perhaps than that I am going to die. Though the thought that I am going to die pretty damn soon is the pits on some grey days. I haven't had enough of life yet and I want to experience the future of my family and friends, especially the grandchildren's.

Almost as worrying is the knowledge that I may not have the final say in how I am going to die. I know it cannot always be arranged and all sorts of circumstances will interfere, but dying at home is far more natural. And it is surely time for more progress to be made on ensuring the individual's right to end their own life.

An indication of this fear of death occurred during an incident that cropped up as Geoff was living his last weeks. He needed a special mattress. The nurse called with it the next morning and it was a single one. So sleeping next to Geoff would have meant me lying down low with him lying up high. Talking as we lay next to each other was still possible, though Geoff's voice was very weak. But at different heights it would not be.

I asked if they could get us a double mattress. They looked gob-smacked, as they hadn't ever been asked for one before. They didn't think there would be one, but they'd find out. The next morning, our squeaky gate announced the arrival of our nurses, who were carrying a double mattress, still in its plastic wrappings. It had never been used, as nobody had ever asked for it. We all loved that moment.

So our close communication continued. We had slipped into being the new age oldies. And I hope there will be plenty of other 'oldies' with a need for that mattress.

During his final weeks, Geoff asked the Reverend Raymond Hughes to come and visit us as he had a favour to ask. He was very ill by that stage and so we all, including Raymond's bubbly wife Sue, gathered around the bed and Geoff asked Raymond would he conduct – if this would not go against the grain – Geoff's funeral in Sion chapel in our village, Llanrhaeadr Ym Mochnant? And, if so, would

Raymond conduct it with the minimum mention of God, as Geoff was not a believer in him, but he did have rapport with the moral basis of the Bible that he had been brought up on, and so wanted to have a service in a church. Raymond lightly pointed out that he'd do his best to respect Geoff's views but Geoff must also understand that we – and he – would be in God's house and God had to be properly thanked. It was agreed; and afterwards Sue and I had a hug and a cry outside the front door, when Geoff's energy had run out and we left him, such a very small figure by now, in the bed. Nothing so outspoken about dying had happened before to Raymond and Sue. Nor since, they have said.

And then we asked Eluned Jones the conductor of the Tanat Dyffryn Choir (the choir of which I am a proud President), if she would come up so that Geoff could request the choir for the service. Yes, she'd ask and she thought most of them would, she added reassuringly. And what hymns would he like to choose? A marvellous Welsh hymn in the minor key, *Calgari*; and then, because of all the rugby matches he'd been to, the emotional *Cwm Rhondda*: 'Guide me, oh Thou great Jehovah'. On the day of the funeral service the choir sang as if their hearts would burst, and then mine did.

There was one strange thing. As Geoff lost weight he looked more like the twenty-year-old I had fallen in love with once upon a time, so that when he died I could only remember our early years for ages after, which was achingly romantic and almost too much to stand, but was perhaps a necessary part of grieving.

What has helped me a lot with my grieving was being able to talk to friends who had been through a loss. The way you are helped by your friends is astonishing. Are we more frank about it than people used to be? It seems to me that my mother's generation didn't quite go in for much counselling with friends. Well, she didn't. Anyway there wasn't much of it around then – not even professionally in the way there is today. My friends were practical when talking about grief and pointed out that the second year is so much better than the first and the third, unexpectedly, reverts to being a bit tricky and tense. It was also vaguely comforting to be told that you don't get over it but you do learn to get used to it, to live with it.

You need courage and you also need to be patient with yourself. You have to embrace your grief as an expression of your love. I know there is a fear that if you start crying when you are on your own, there is nothing to stop you. But I found I wore myself out. Give in to it when it overcomes you. I'm sorry to say, though, that it doesn't really get better for ages. And grief arrives without warning even now. You do learn how to cope with it and not mind that it takes you over. I liken it to getting into very cold water. Once you accustom yourself to it you are fine. And, gradually, you don't need to mourn so much and memories take over and hopefully life intrudes. And you get on with living and – yes, I will admit it – you start to enjoy a curious unwanted freedom. A bit of a new you.

For instance, I have no one to quarrel with! This is quite a revelation to me. How did Geoff put up with my bad moods? My sulks? I long for him to come back and see if I would still be this new angelic being. Or would I, with someone around again, start to bicker and have bad moods and complain that we had no friends and never did anything. And why were we living in the country? And please would he mind making supper sometimes and why didn't he think up some meals instead of leaving it all to me?

When you are on your own you don't have to stick to a timetable. Meals are when you are hungry. Meals – what are they? Food that you eat out of the frying pan standing up in the kitchen watching the birds on the wall outside eating the breakfast you have left for them.

I have not caught on to the knack of making a meal for myself and sitting down and enjoying the whole ritual – not quite. My mother said she made herself lay the table and then she would prop up a book against the vase of flowers and eat a proper meal that way. Or she'd have a radio on in front of her. Or she'd do the crossword in the *Daily Mirror*. She admitted she soon got sick of this and found she couldn't be bothered to lay the table for one and became more slovenly with just a plate on her lap in front of the telly, for, it was possible, presumably, when eating in this way, to delude yourself into thinking you were sharing a meal with someone.

When you are a loner, you are free to go where you like when you like. So the new lonelier, freer me is able to go and stay with friends when they are ill and help look after them – just like that. Geoff wouldn't have stopped his Florence Nightingale going, but she would have felt guilty leaving him on his own. Would have avoided it more times than not and the single friend wouldn't have looked in her direction to help out when she was part of a couple either.

Because a lot of my friends are around my age and on their own, I have found that I have company for going out on jaunts and holidays. But I only discovered *that* when I was able to pluck up the courage and gain confidence in myself and be bold enough to ask. It was quite a big step forward for me since, before Geoff died, he and I did most things together and I never had to ask.

I am lucky too that not all my friends are as old as me, and I have good friends of all ages who are willing to come out and play. And thank heavens my sons and their wives are my best friends, too. I'm down on my knees in gratitude about that.

I was warned that a woman on her own isn't asked out to dinner parties, but haven't found this to be the case. There are plenty of singles around us (men and women) so I've had no trouble with that. But I don't ever go out to eat on my own. Waste of money. And, apart from that, I can't get up the nerve to sit over a meal in a restaurant on my tod. I've felt lonely and self-conscious when I tried. I thought everyone was pitying me for being on the shelf.

It is not an easy transition to make – to become single after so long. And the change affects everything; from how and where I eat to how I dress. I have a feeling I am slightly more careful about how I look now. My style has changed a bit because I don't feel beautiful anymore without him around to make me feel that I am. I also dress for my own pleasure since I am not out to entrap a chap as no chap wants a seventy-year-old to have and to hold from this day forward since there may not be many more days to look forward to and increasingly the days might be creaky anyway. Old men want younger women because – apart from anything else – they are strong enough to look after them, I am pretty sure. It is still an unfair fact that old men can pick and choose far more than old women even in this more enlightened time.

I know there is only a short time left and I am trying my hardest not to dwell on it. My granddaughter talked to me the other day about how exciting it'll be to have the Olympics in London. And I said what I vowed I wouldn't ever say: 'If I am still alive by then, my darling.' Her face looked quite distraught for a moment and I wondered was it a good thing to warn the young that you will not be around forever?

I do try to grasp the freedom of my seventies with open arms and even though I am sadder and no wiser I feel very open to life, perhaps because there is so little of it left. I have never wanted to grow old disgracefully. I don't want to start behaving any more 'disgracefully' than I have acted in the past. Nor any the less, I hastily add, though chance would be a fine thing.

So here I am, an 'incompleat woman', though a bit more complete since the arrival of Iris, my third granddaughter, who arrived after her grandfather had died.

There is one marvellous perk about living on my own in a stunning part of remote Wales: nothing impedes my view of the star-studded sky. Now, if we come from star matter, as some people say we do, and if we return to star matter, as some people say we do, then I am in frequent touch with Geoff and one day will join him up there with the myriad of stars. What an ending... if it could be true.

Love Bade Me Welcome

Anne Rowe

My mother was seventy-nine when I came along. It was a blistering day in August 2001, and I had recently turned forty-nine. I was cleaning the upstairs windows in the terraced cottage we had just bought in Wales, and heard a knocking at the door. My husband called up to announce the arrival of our next-door neighbour, and I hurried down the spiral stairs to meet her. Framed in the doorway was my brand new mother, carrying a tray laden with iced orange squash and glasses, 'In case your fridge isn't working yet.' She introduced herself as Eiddwen. While her brown eyes radiated a warmth that placed her quickly near my heart, her accent located her even more precisely. She came from Ebbw Vale, the valley adjoining Tredegar, where I was born, and our shared heritage, the Chapel-going, hymn-singing, Welsh Valleys culture that nurtured us both, was, I'm sure, a form of emotional shorthand that bound us together from that moment on.

My real mother had died more than twenty-five years before, and now I no longer missed having one; perhaps I even felt relieved to be free of the responsibility. I'd certainly grown used to the lack of a maternal influence and no longer mourned it. I'd been well consoled, anyway, for the loss by my father, whom I adored, and who lived to be ninety. But, now, looking back, something crucial must have been missing from my life: the child inside was still longing for unconditional love and acceptance; I'd forgotten how to give the love a daughter gives a mother and must have been, without ever being aware of it, emotionally isolated. Living most of my adult life in England had only intensified that isolation: there, I was suspicious of being ridiculed; in Wales, people were suspicious of my ridiculing them. In Surrey I was immediately identified as an 'outsider' – the first question I tended to be asked was 'Where are you from?' (My accent has been identified variously as Polish, Irish, Geordie, and most gratifyingly, Swedish.) In Wales, on the other hand, the minute I opened my mouth, a chorus of 'Well, there's posh you are' could make me red with embarrassment. I belonged nowhere.

My feelings about Wales had become ambivalent – sentimentalised and stigmatised equally. We were settled in Surrey at the time I met Eiddwen, but I had just inherited my father's terraced house in Tredegar. We decided to sell and buy a bigger family home for weekends in the area of the Brecon Beacons National Park. Retaining a home in Wales was only partially to do with reclaiming a Welshness that was being eroded by a middle-class English lifestyle (I taught at university; my children went to private schools; I hosted the ubiquitous dinner parties, frequented the opera and art galleries and even, God forbid, employed a cleaning lady). The move stemmed more from practicality: we needed a regular base from where we could comfortably look after my husband's ageing parents at weekends.

At the time I didn't think about 'belonging' in Wales – I was convinced then that I belonged out of it. I still cherished my memories of the close community, the extended family, and the landscape. We supported Welsh rugby, joined Welsh expatriate events in London and had wanted our sons (named Ieuan and Gareth) to be proud of their Welsh heritage. But we were all Anglo-Welsh, not really Welsh any more. I'd grown used to the privacy afforded by English reserve, and my sentimental memories of Welsh day-to-day existence were alien to my life now. I couldn't contemplate living permanently within the claustrophobic world of intrusive, well-meaning neighbours or indeed the oppressive geography of the Valleys that, viewed from what had become my outsider's perspective, felt stultifying. I couldn't go back and didn't want to. My Welshness was useful mostly as a conversation piece – it was rather picturesque at dinner parties to have a strong cultural heritage, and the more working class the better. Working class roots proved that successes were earned; they announced a lack of pretension and demonstrated 'character'. At the same time, however, the identity I'd established for myself – accomplished, well-educated, successful – made me feel a fraud. It had to be luck; I wasn't born into this life and never felt deserving of it.

But the real luck came with Eiddwen, who responded only to the motherless child from Tredegar – she had no knowledge or conception of the other me ('I knew you were "one of us"' she will say); her unlimited capacity for love and her innocent expectations of who I was tugged and tugged me back to my roots. A few hours after the arrival of the iced orange squash (I hadn't tasted that for years – only sparkling water, please, on a hot day in Surrey), the same tray came back again bearing a steaming pot of tea and a plate of Welsh cakes. The nurturing had begun. That plate has traversed the threshold a thousand times since. It's been the bearer of a variety of Welsh cakes, sometimes with jam, sometimes lemon curd, while other times it carries buttery shortcake with caramel and smooth milk chocolate, or strawberry-coloured cakes coaxed into a pyramid shape, slithered with jam, dusted with fresh coconut and flourished with a cherry. Occasionally there will be banana bread, or flapjacks, or Bara Brith. When I'm poorly there's a dish of warm baked egg custard, still quaking and dusted with nutmeg. This is the food that faddish diets have demonised, and I've avoided as assiduously as the plague for the past twenty years. Now, during the week, I'm more abstemious than ever – but only to save myself for Fridays. Eiddwen's is my first port of call, and with the smell of baking in the air, I get a much-needed *cwtch* and then the cakes are brought out of the kitchen. There's a square of kitchen paper balanced on top, and oh, the joy of lifting it off. On the long journey from London, the thrill of expectation and the mouth-watering lingering over the possibilities is almost as good as the real thing – and I know I shall not want.

We loved each other. And it wasn't long before I found myself at a Cymanfa Ganu that happened to fall on a weekend. I phoned a friend in the week who said, 'See you Saturday.' 'Where am I going?' I asked. 'Llangattock Baptist Chapel. With Eiddwen.' I was amused at myself as we walked through the door (half an hour early to get a good seat near the front) – it seemed a ridiculous thing, at 7.30pm on a warm, summer Saturday evening, to be singing hymns instead of sipping Pimms. But I was learning all sorts of things about myself: the smell, the taste even, of ancient, dusty pews and hymn-books caught in the back of my throat, then the hissing and pumping of the organ as it struck up the first hymn sent me back to my Sunday School days and conjured up childhood horrors with remarkable vividness. Albert Jones, for example, the finger-wagging Deacon of Bethania Congregational Chapel, Tredegar: 'God is watching you.' As a child I was guilt-ridden and paranoid at the thought and I remain so.

I knew I could still remember the odd hymn tune such as *Jesus Loves Me* and, for some reason, *When the Roll is Called up Yonder*, but I was convinced I'd utterly forgotten most of the many Sankey hymns I'd learned by heart. I hadn't. They'd been safely stored as saved data, word for word, ready to be resurrected at the first clap of the bellows. As Eiddwen struck up beside me, verse after verse proceeded mechanically from my mouth. It was a distinctly unnerving almost schizophrenic feeling that some child-demon inside was holding forth quite independently of the adult who had walked in. Three or four verses and the chorus (sung twice with vigour at the end) flowed from my mouth like ghostly, undulating ribbons – and word perfect, if you please. Even more disturbing was the fact that I remembered the numbers in the hymn book: *Count Your Blessings* (745); *Beulah Land* (944); *What a Friend We Have in Jesus* (Eiddwen's favourite, 319), and (this one still moves me to tears) *Just as I am without one plea, but that thy blood was shed for me. And that Thou bid'st me come to Thee, O Lamb of God, I come* (473). I was flummoxed, though, at the final *Till We Meet Again*. The words had vanished and

Eiddwen glanced sideways at the sudden silence. I got her 'big eyes' – the sort of glare that appears when I'm being told off. Next morning, the words had been carefully written out and put through my door. So all's well, and in future I can finish with a flourish, as indeed can whoever burgled my English home last year. The little folded paper Eiddwen had written on was tucked into my jewellery box with all my other treasures. Somewhere in Surrey a burglar stalks the streets with his swag, singing, 'till we meet at Jesus' feet.'

And so I was integrated back into the culture I had thought antiquated and redundant in my life. But Eiddwen had not only restored my soul, she had also led me into the paths of righteousness. The responsibility of having a mother to account to has made me more moral. When I recently reversed into a Mercedes (causing only *very* minor damage), I left a note on the windscreen with apologies, name and telephone number. My English friends thought such scruples were mildly insane. It was not fear of CCTV that brought about such integrity; it was the thought of facing Eiddwen at the weekend. And neither, I find, can I waste the merest morsel of food ('if you had lived through the war, my love…'). After years of carelessly discarding half-eaten meals, of over-providing by the fridgeful, and exercising excess in all things culinary (my answer to a successful dinner party has always been to throw money at it and thus ensure a good impression), now the soggiest left-over parsnip has to be made useful. Will it go in a soup? Will it make a pie? Can it be reheated?

A more rigorous conscience has brought the most surprising rewards. On a recent visit to Covent Garden to see *Rigoletto*, my thoughts drifted to my music teacher at school. His name was Mr Martin and he was an exacting and brilliant choir master. I realised how his teaching had stood me in such good stead – my pleasure in singing must, in some part, have stemmed from his 'training'. Wallowing in the emotion generated by the music, I resolved to write a letter of thanks to Mr Herbert Martin. Many such resolutions in my life have soon been swallowed up by more pressing demands, but now I knew what Eiddwen would expect of me. 'Sir' was, by all accounts, thrilled to have been so fondly remembered when he received my letter and the programme from *Rigoletto* I had also enclosed. He died shortly afterwards.

My real mother's quite sudden death came soon after I became a mother myself. Daughterly responsibilities were abruptly severed when I lost her and when I still needed some-one to be responsible to, as well as for. My husband's closeness to my father had given my father the son he had always wanted, so my duties there had been diluted. Eiddwen indulges me in a way my own mother never could. That my mother loved me I'm sure, but she was nearing forty when I was born, and was never able to express her love in the way Eiddwen is able to. In the week, when I call Eiddwen, she always ends with 'love you lots' and I know the sentiment is real. When I put down the phone, I try to remember if I ever heard my real mother say such a thing, and I'm sure I didn't. She was not affectionate to me and died before I had the chance to find out why that might have been. Eiddwen has allowed me to be the daughter I never had the chance to be, and has invited me not only to remember but to relive my childhood dependencies and responsibilities by indulging me, and at the same time expecting the best of me.

Now, I think her influence is leading me to wonder if remnants of the faith that was ingrained in that blood-and-thunder Nonconformist childhood are still lurking alongside the words of the hymns and the craving for nursery food that Eiddwen has so unexpectedly resurrected. She believes in God and never misses Chapel on Sundays. Her dearly loved Jack is buried in the graveyard behind her house and I know she believes that she'll be with him again. My own faith hasn't quite simmered into fashionable cynicism, but it has certainly ebbed. I've always kept guiltily, though, a print of a painting by William Holman Hunt in my Surrey home. It's called *The Light of The World*, and it's a kitsch stereotypical picture of Christ standing at a doorway. This Christ looks just like the one I became acquainted with at Sunday School – he carries a lantern which lights up a kindly face that looks troubled – (disappointed with me, I've often thought). Over the years, this picture of a benign and loving Christ, come to save a lost soul, has been relegated from room to room. Twenty years ago it was in the dining room (God knows what the dinner party guests thought), then it was shifted to my (less public) study, and now, something of an embarrassment, but for some reason indispensible, it resides in the downstairs loo. It has an accompanying text from Revelations: 'Behold I stand at the door and knock; if any man hear my voice and open the door I will come to him and will sup with him and he with me.' I used to hanker for a knock at *my* door – it seemed it would never come, and while I've had nothing of the kind of revelation Holman Hunt intends to inspire, I'm certainly more alert to coincidences.

There have been two of late: for many of the years that I have specialised in the work of Iris Murdoch, I'd meant to trace a phrase that is a motif in her novels: 'there are principalities and powers.' All I knew was that it had Biblical origins. Then Eiddwen kept for me the order of service from a neighbour's memorial service. One of the readings was from Romans (Chapter 8 verse 28-39). 'You'll know that one,' she said, but I murmured some excuse for not recognising it. She went for her Bible and pointed to the penultimate verse which she said was the one I would be most likely to recognise: 'For I am persuaded, that neither death, nor life, nor angels, nor principalities, nor powers, nor things present, nor things to come, nor height, nor depth, nor any other creature, shall be able to separate us from the love of God.' The next coincidence came on a Saturday morning when I had to get back to the university and went in to say goodbye. For no particular reason, she gave me a tiny silver angel on a chain, and when she said that I was her angel I remember thinking that no, she was mine. Later in the day, at the Centre for Iris Murdoch Studies, as I was fondling the angel, I glanced towards the annotated books from Murdoch's Oxford library displayed in a cabinet. My eyes rested on *The Life of St Teresa of Avila* in which Murdoch had scribbled, 'If the angels are sinless how can they be less than God, how can they not be God?' I have no idea what I think this means or what I want it to mean. But I know that I can see connections in things that before would have passed me by, and I'm thinking about them.

Recently, after carols and hymn-singing in Wales and a more than usually reflective drive back, I even dusted down my Bible and flicked through randomly. It fell open at the Book of Ruth. It's a beautiful story, about Naomi, who has two sons and, eventually, two daughters-in-law. Both sons die and Naomi tells her daughters-in-law that they must return to their own mothers. Orpah returns, but Ruth loves Naomi, and refuses. When Ruth remarries, Naomi becomes nurse to her son – so that Ruth in effect replaces Naomi's lost son. To me, the story redefines natural bonds: it suggests that love, forged outside familial or cultural bonds, can be just as powerful and lasting as those forged within them. I understand that a large part of the person I am is the product of the forces that shaped me as a child, and that they've survived more than half a lifetime of cultural exile. They were always there, just resting, ready to surface given the right trigger. So the weekend trips have evolved from 'going to Wales' to 'going home'. There are penalties of course. On Sunday evenings as we drive away, leaving Eiddwen behind, I'm reminded of saying goodbye to my father years ago and feel again the wrench between wanting to be there, and at the same time wanting to be back in London with my work and my friends. The discomfort won't go away until we cross Richmond Bridge and I see the lights from the bars and the restaurants glitter on the surface of the Thames. Only then do I consider myself 'home'. But I know that the next journey back across the Severn Bridge will produce that sense of 'home' again in Wales.

I'm destined for a life of cultural schizophrenia, of journeying East to West and back again. Because, for whatever time is left, I want, like Ruth, to be as much as I can with my adopted mother: 'for wither thou goest I will go: and where thou lodgest I will lodge; thy people shall be my people, and thy God, my God.' I always slide the window down in the car to catch the last glimpse as we drive away. She won't go in until we are out of sight and will stand, framed in the light of the doorway, waving. I wave back, my arm out of the car window and strain forward to get the last glimpse in the wing mirror, unable to take my eyes off her, blurred by my tears. Just after Christmas, as I watched her when we left last time, it struck me: it had come – that knock on the door.

Biographies

Robyn ap Gwilym is an unradical feminist who enjoys watching *Buffy the Vampire Slayer*. Robyn loves dressing up, dancing and socialising and swings both ways. Robyn enjoys swimming in the sea, the calming effects of Prozac, and sunsets on Denmark Hill.

Patricia Duncker was born in the West Indies and still dreams about heat, earthquakes and hurricanes. She is the author of four novels which can be read as route maps for her travels: *Hallucinating Foucault* (1996), which is a Big Gay Read set mostly in France; *James Miranda Barry* (1999), which starts off in rural England, circles the Mediterranean and returns to Jamaica, to the very house where she once lived; *The Deadly Space Between* (2002), a satanic thriller that hurtles through Germany, pauses by Lake Constance and ends poised above the glaciers of Chamonix, and most recently *Miss Webster and*

Cherif (2006), where she settles not so peacefully into an English village then heads off into the desert wastes of the Sahara. When she's not on the road Patricia lives in Aberystwyth.

Holly Howitt is the author of two novels, many microfictions and infinite lies. This is her first non-fiction piece to be published, but her debut novel is in the publishing pipeline (wherever that may be). Holly lives in Cardiff but still has nightmares about the open spaces of rural Clwyd, where she grew up.

Layla Jabero has recently been signed to play midfield for the Reading Royal Ladies, having previously played for Premier League Southern Division rivals Brighton and Hove.

Catherine Johnson was brought up in North London. Her parents are from Wales and Jamaica. Catherine studied film at St Martin's School of Art where her final piece was a remake of Rapunzel. She has worked as a horse wrangler, as writer-in-residence at Holloway Prison and was Reader-in-Residence at the Royal Festival Hall. She also writes for film and TV.

Liz Jones lives in a tiny hamlet in the foothills of the Cambrian Mountains with her husband, two daughters and five semi-feral cats. After wasting half her adult life in unsuitable jobs in London, she now works at home as a copywriter, journalist and, in recent years, as a playwright. Her children's play *The Trainee Fairy Godmother* was recently produced by Cardigan Youth Theatre. Now she's studying for an MA in Scriptwriting at the University of Glamorgan and is writing *The Chequered Angel*, a play about eighteenth-century 'punk' poet and celebrity, Ann Yearsley.

Sadie Kiernan was born in 1971 and moved to Wales as a toddler, then back to London as an adult. Despite starting three degrees, she ended up in Sales and Administration but along the way has worked as a librarian for Anton Mosimann, helped run a boxing gym, and started her own record label whilst on dialysis. She DJs and works for Refuge: For Women and Children, Against Domestic Violence and is an excellent cook.

Carol Lee is an established author, journalist and a playwright. Born in Carmarthenshire, she spent much of her childhood in Africa. Of her eight published books, the latest three, *To Die For*, *Crooked Angels* and *A Child Called Freedom*, all have Welsh/African themes. Living in London, she copes with the tomfoolery of Life in general and Publishers in particular by playing tennis and dancing tango – although not at the same time. On regular visits to Wales she walks by the sea in Cefn Sidan and Llansteffan.

Caryl Lewis is a native of Ceredigion and writes novels, TV scripts and children's books full-time. She believes Tunnock's Tea Cakes to be an essential aid to writing and likes talking to her cat Nokia. She is shacked up with a handsome shepherd and lives halfway up a mountain. Her most successful book to date is *Martha Jac a Sianco*, which won the Welsh Book of the Year Award 2005 and is due to appear in English in 2007.

Hayley Long is a part-time teacher, occasional editor and sometime DJ, as well as the author of two novels: *Fire and Water* and *Kilburn Hoodoo*. She has been sacked and re-instated several times as the manager of Aberystwyth Town FC, but only within the confines of Championship Manager 2005.

Jo Mazelis has published two collections of short stories, *Diving Girls*, which was shortlisted for Commonwealth Best First Book and Welsh Book of the Year, and *Circle Games*, which was longlisted for Welsh Book of the Year. She is the only writer to have won a prize in the Rhys Davies Short Story Competition three times. Born in Swansea, she worked in London in the late eighties and early nineties for several magazines, including *Women's Review*, *Spare Rib*, *City Limits* and *Everywoman*. She has exhibited her photographs in London and Swansea. She has an MA in the Diversity of Contemporary Literature from the University of Wales, Swansea, as well as qualifications in art and design. A selection of her stories, *Forbidden Fruit,* is due to be published in Denmark in spring 2007.

Mavis Nicholson – Mavis Mainwaring – was born in 1930 in Briton Ferry, South Wales. After Swansea University she worked as a copywriter in several big advertising agencies in London. She was forty when she got into afternoon television presenting a daily programme hosted by women: *Good Afternoon*. She went on to work for Jeremy Isaacs on Channel 4 in *Mavis on Four*. She wrote columns for magazines such as *Nova* and for the *Evening Standard* and is the author of three books: *Help Yourself* (a practical advice book), *Martha, Jane and Me* (about her girlhood in Wales) and *What did you do in the War, Mummy?* (a book of interviews with active women in the last world war).

Now she does some occasional television work, is the agony aunt in *The Oldie* magazine and edits the local community paper, *The Chronicle*.

Anne Rowe is a lecturer, editor and writer. Born in Tredegar, in the South Wales Valleys, she lived there until she married and moved to London. She is now a specialist on the work of Iris Murdoch, about whom she has written and edited books and articles, and is a lecturer and Director of the Centre for Iris Murdoch Studies at Kingston University. She divides her time between Crickhowell in Powys and Kingston in Surrey. In Wales she enjoys singing hymns; in London, she likes to sip Pimms. She still doesn't know which she prefers. She is interested in Welsh art and artists and intends, one day, to write on links between the poetry of RS Thomas and the paintings of Kyffin Williams.

Charmian Savill was once called 'that sex goddess from Wales' by Howard Barker. In her spare time she obsesses over her garden and cookery books. Charmian has written plays and performance poetry; directs plays that are poetic, and adapts poetry for the stage. In 2007 she will direct Gwyneth Lewis' *Y Llofrudd Iaith* and Nigel Wells' *Gwaliadir* for the Lurking Truth theatre company. Her favourite moments are listening to her daughter Isabel's soul/blues/jazz compositions and watching her son dance. She is regularly seen running out of her house screaming at fat cats who stalk her precious wild birds. Her day job is teaching at the University of Wales Aberystwyth's Television and Theatre Studies department, on the Welsh-language side.

Rachel Trezise is a writer and journalist. Her work includes the autobiographical novel *In and Out of the Goldfish Bowl* and the short story collection *Fresh Apples,* which won the EDS Dylan Thomas Prize in 2006. In an attempt to rid small children of the ill-effects of Barbie dolls, she collects them and hides them in the spare room. Rachel lives in the Rhondda Valley.

Rose Wilkins writes teen chick-lit and works in publishing, where she fully supports the axiom that all authors whinge and all editors are over-worked. Her latest book, *Wishful Thinking*, will be published by Macmillan in spring 2007, and her not-so-chick-lit writing has featured in *Poetry Wales* and the *Literary Review*. She has an unhealthy obsession with peanut butter milkshakes, *Mansfield Park* and Kevin Spacey.

Acknowledgements

Thank you firstly to the contributors, for their imagination, verve and commitment to the project. Thanks also to Eleanor and Sam for the lovely cover and to Gwen for her insights and focus and Richard and Dom for their energy and enthusiasm. Also thanks to Lloyd and Gina.

And to my dear friends and family: Kirsti Bohata, Susan Doyon, Carla von der Becke, Polly Thorpe, Hester Jewitt, Tamsin Deuchars, Claudia Townsend, Meg Jensen, Pam Kiernan, Ann Smith, Sharon Young, Blake Morrison, Brian Cathcart and Ceilidh Chaplin.

diverse probing
profound **urban**
epic **comic**
rural savage
new writing

Independent
Presses
Management

INPRESS

www.inpressbooks.co.uk

gwales.com

Llyfrau ar-lein

Books on-line

PARTHIAN

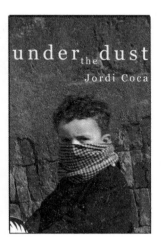

parthianbooks.co.uk